A WOMAN

EDITED BY TERRY PRONE

First published in 1994 by
Martello Books
An imprint of Mercier Press
16 Hume Street Dublin 2

Trade enquiries to Mercier Press
PO Box 5, 5 French Church Street,
Cork

A Martello Original

Foreword © Terry Prone 1994
The acknowledgements page is an
extension of this copyright notice

ISBN 1 86023 006 7

10 9 8 7 6 5 4 3 2 1

A CIP record for this title is available
from the British Library

Cover design by Niamh Sharkey
Set by Richard Parfrey in Avant
Garde and Caslon 10/15
Printed in Ireland by ColourBooks,
Baldoyle Industrial Estate, Dublin 13

CONTENTS

CECIL FRANCIS ALEXANDER   ONCE IN ROYAL DAVID'S CITY   V

INTRODUCTION   TERRY PRONE   VII

VAL MULKERNS   HOME FOR CHRISTMAS   9

MAEVE BINCHY   CHRISTMAS WITH THE O'CONNORS   19

ANNE DEVLIN   THE JOURNEY TO SOMEWHERE ELSE   26

PATRICIA LYNCH   LAST BUS FOR CHRISTMAS   46

TERRY PRONE   BUTTERFLY CHRISTMAS   55

CELIA SALKELD   MARIE-CLARE   65

PEIG SAYERS   CHRISTMAS FAR FROM HOME   80

MAIRE WALSH   ON THE SECOND DAY OF CHRISTMAS   87

MOY McCRORY   WHITE CHRISTMAS, 1953   94

E. SOMERVILLE & M. ROSS   OWENEEN THE SPRAT   111

MARY BECKETT   ANTI-SANTY   131

VICTORIA WHITE   ELECTRICITY   133

GERALDINE DESMOND   YOUR MOTHER OWNED CHRISTMAS   139

MARY ROSE CALLAGHAN   I HATE CHRISTMAS!   146

ANNIE M. P. SMITHSON   CHRISTMAS IN OLD DUBLIN   156

JENNIFER JOHNSTON   A PROPOSAL   160

MAURA LAVERTY   THE DEAD MARKET   164

KATE CRUISE O'BRIEN   THE AUSTRALIAN WOMAN   174

HONOR DUFF   FROST FIGURES   188

BIOGRAPHICAL NOTES   200

ACKNOWLEDGEMENTS   203

This collection is dedicated to David Marcus, whose enthusiasm and rigour have been central to the development of so many short story writers and poets.

ONCE IN ROYAL DAVID'S CITY

CECIL FRANCIS ALEXANDER

Once in Royal David's City
Stood a lonely cattle shed,
Where a Mother laid her Baby
In a manger for His bed;
Mary was that Mother mild,
Jesus Christ her little child.

He came down to earth from Heaven
Who is God and Lord of all,
And his shelter was a stable,
And his cradle was a stall;
With the poor, and mean, and lowly,
Lived on earth our Saviour Holy.

And through all His wondrous Childhood,
He would honour and obey,
Love, and watch the lowly Maiden,
In whose gentle arms He lay;
Christian children all must be
Mild, obedient, good as He.

For He is our childhood's pattern,
Day by day like us he grew.
He was little, weak, and helpless,
Tears and smile like us he knew
And He feeleth for our sadness,
And He shareth in our gladness.

And our eyes at last shall see Him,
Through His own redeeming love,
For that Child so dear and gentle
Is our Lord in Heav'n above;
And He leads His children on
To the place where He is gone.

Not in that poor lowly stable,
With the oxen standing by,
We shall see Him; but in heaven,
Set at God's right hand on high;
When like stars His children crown'd
All in white shall wait around.
Amen

Poems, 1896

FOREWORD

TERRY PRONE

Every year it resurfaces, that 'study' showing Christmas to be the most depressing time of the year, provocative of family conflict, marital disruption and a raised level of suicide.

It isn't true.

That 'study' doesn't exist. But the factoid satisfies a need to see Christmas as more complicated than it looks at first glance. The same need gives rise to the annual agonising that, somehow, we are losing touch with the essence of the feast. That we are commercialising it out of existence.

'It's supposed to be for *children*,' the advocates of this view-point say.

But if Christmas is particularly important to children, it's arguably of equal importance to writers. For writers, the imperative is to get past the tinselled surface of the season to something more significant. The task, for a writer, is greatly facilitated by the centrifugal force Christmas exerts on family life, pulling generations together, bringing wanderers home and subjecting all to a spinning pressure of spending, of eating, drinking, aching expectations and annual dismay.

This collection of writings by and about women invites the reader to accommodate a huge variety of Christmases, past and present, factual and fictional. There is the fairy-tale approach of Patricia Lynch to contrast with the sad observer stance of Peig Sayers and the harshly wistful viewpoint of

Celia Salkeld. There are stories from writers published in the last couple of decades, like Mary Rose Callaghan and Honor Rynne, about families learning from each other during the festive season, and there are pieces from writers sadly unfamiliar to many readers today, like Maura Laverty.

There are moments in every Christmas season when the excitement dies down and a book is a refuge and a refreshment. *A Woman's Christmas* sets out to be both. And to underline that the continuum of Christmas tends to be lovingly handed on through the female line.

HOME FOR CHRISTMAS

VAL MULKERNS

The Christmas of that year stands out in my mind with a kind of finality. I was fourteen, and abruptly at the end of the holidays some soft, almost physical appendage of childhood seems to have fallen away, like the tail off a tadpole, and I would never be quite the same again.

My father came in a hired car to collect me from my aunt's house where I was boarded during the school term. He was ushered up in state to what they called 'the room' which was now several degrees below zero. My aunt took from his numbed hands the bright bundle of Christmas presents from Mother and fussed him into an armchair by the stark fireplace, black except for a paper fan made from newspapers which was presumably intended as a decoration. In a few freezing moments the small underpaid servant girl (recently acquired from the orphanage) came in carrying a lighted oil stove which was sometimes used in the bedrooms if anybody was sick. Those were the cold war-time years when only the poor, with tiny houses, could really keep warm. But no house I had ever known was as miserably cold as this handsome farmhouse a few miles from the marble city of Kilkenny.

'Thanks very much, Bernie,' said my father to the girl. 'And how are you this fine hearty morning?'

'Grand, sir, thanks.' When my aunt turned to get the whiskey he slipped Bernie a ten-shilling note, winking

9

elaborately and motioning her to silence. She skipped away beaming, closing the door behind her.

'Are you sure now, Daniel, you wouldn't like the fire lit? 'Twouldn't be any trouble and indeed it would give that bone-lazy young one something to do.'

'I can't stay too long, so don't trouble yourself, Ellen.'

'Anyway,' said my aunt, 'sure the sun is so strong 'twould likely put the fire out.' She handed him his whiskey and I knew by the tight curl of his lip as he raised his glass to drink her health that he was trying to smother a laugh. Later he would tell my mother about this – Ellen's latest scientific discovery – and they would roar laughing together.

'Won't you join me, Ellen, and the festive season that's in it?'

'Sure maybe a taste of the sherry wine would be no harm and me with a cold,' my aunt agreed.

'Do you all the good in the world, Ellen,' said my father heartily, and though I could see his throat stretching for the bite of the whiskey, he waited until she had filled her glass. He was just about to give the wish when Ellen thought better of her self-indulgence and poured half of the sherry back into the bottle, spilling some in the process. She was no doubt remembering how near Christmas was, and how as many as six distant cousins might drop in over the season.

'Your good health, Ellen, and here's a happy Christmas to us all and many of them!'

'Amen to that,' said my aunt, taking a sip and then watching nervously as my father joyously swallowed half his drink in one go and smacked his lips genially after it.

'Good stuff, Ellen. The best. Warm the cockles of your

heart!' and the practised charm of his best professional smile brought a slight response even from Ellen though you could see that a smile of any sort hurt her, as the effort to walk hurts a rheumatic.

'Tell me,' said my aunt grudgingly, 'how was it Peg couldn't have come over with you and you with the car got and all?'

'Work, Ellen, work. Christmas party dresses for gay young things who have been saving their clothes coupons which ought to have been spent on good woollen stockings to keep the cold out. All sorts of refurbished finery for the old – overcoats "turned" and that sort of thing. She said she'd have to let some of her clients down if she took the whole day off to come here. Assured me you'd understand.'

'And so I do,' Ellen conceded. 'How is she keeping, tell me?'

'Splendid form, thank God. In fact, hopelessly elevated at the thought of seeing our young friend here after three long months. I must say, Ellen, he's looking a credit to your good care. A credit.'

Head down, I continued my perusal of the mouldering fox in the glass case, an unfailing delight because in strong winter sunlight like this you could see that really the taxidermist hadn't done such a good job. If you watched one patch of fur closely until your eyes ached, you became aware that infinitesimal life was moving along each stiffened hair, minute flaky things like the inhabitants of old damp books. No wonder. You could see the unused furniture gently steaming in the slight combined warmth of sun and oil heater. The windows of this room were always kept hermetically sealed except in high summer.

'He's a sturdy lad enough,' my aunt agreed, 'and a great help to us at the harvest.' This was dangerous talk although she was too stupid to be aware of it. My father might easily enquire why I hadn't been at school then. But my aunt's tongue, loosened by the sherry, ran on. 'Your Danny reminds me something wonderful of Martin, you know. Come over here till you look at him the year before he left the priests' college when we still thought he was going on for a priest.'

My father went at her bidding to the far wall, blotched with damp, whose mud-coloured wallpaper fell in loose folds around the smiling face of my disreputable uncle. The photographer seemed to have caught the moment before a wink. His clerical collar looked like fancy dress and if the family had looked honestly at him they'd have known themselves that he had his own future planned despite them.

'Look at the chin now,' said my aunt, 'and the cock of the head and the way the hair grows over the forehead. The dead spit of Dan. Look up at us now, Danny boy.' I did, and instantly lowered my head again as my father nodded.

'You have a point there, Ellen, no doubt about it.' He had not allowed himself to be separated from his drink, and now swallowed the remainder with relish, maybe for consolation.

'I don't suppose you'd take another drop, Daniel?' said my aunt in the tone of voice that made lady visitors refuse another slice of madeira cake.

'Do you know, I think I will, Ellen – a mere tincture, mind, one for the road. We must be off in a minute or two if we're to be home before dark.'

My aunt poured another half-glass of whiskey and even I

could detect the portentous gloom in her voice when she spoke again. 'We're after getting a Christmas card below from Nellie – would you credit it after all these years?'

'And how is she?' said my father lightly.

'Don't you know well how she is though she never says a word? There was a man from here went working to Boston not long ago – one of the Clearys, I don't know if you remember them? Well, he caught sight of Nellie, not so much changed as you'd think, he said, but the worse for drink in the company of two men outside a public house. Drink is the curse of the world, Daniel, and sure poor Martin himself only for it wouldn't have any wife at all to live on after him and hold his name and ours up to ridicule.'

'As I remember the somewhat distressing story, Ellen, it was *after* Martin had been shipped away by his family that he sought the consolations of alcohol – and later of matrimony.'

'All that's as may be,' said my aunt briskly. 'The fact is the same Nellie is a disgrace to us all and shouldn't use his name at all at all if she had any shame.'

'The name nevertheless *is* hers,' said my father with finality. 'Thank you, Ellen, for the kind drop but we must be off now.'

'You're in a great hurry,' said my aunt slyly. 'You wouldn't let me fill your glass again to keep the cold out, Daniel?'

'I wouldn't, Nellie. My insulation is completed now.' As I went to him he bent to examine the dusty artificial roses in the bowl on the table, into which little sprigs of lurid green celluloid holly had been stuck. 'There's a touch of the artist about you, Ellen,' he said, and I could have cheered at the wickedness of him. 'Before I go won't you allow me to wish a happy Christmas

13

to my niece and nephew, Ellen? Where have you hidden them?'

'Ann and Matthew is below stairs with the young one,' my aunt said, somewhat put out. 'They have a cold on them and we didn't bother cleaning them up today.'

'Nevertheless.' His smile was really quite charming as well as indomitable, and my aunt Ellen reluctantly led the way downstairs. The fact is, he really *liked* children. In the kitchen, glowing with warmth from the unguarded fire, we found Ann wiping her nose on a dirty pinafore and Matthew throwing small pieces of torn-up paper into the fire and watching them roar up the chimney. Bernie made at once for the yard as my aunt appeared.

'I shouldn't do that, Matthew,' my father said, lifting the small boy up in one arm and Ann in the other. 'Little boys who do that have a habit of not growing up.' He smiled at both children and they beamed back with delighted grubby faces. Born long after Aunt Ellen was judged to be past the age for childbearing, they were usually ignored in that house or left to the overworked Bernie to look after. During term-time they were kept clean enough for school but in the holidays nobody bothered with them. My father however worked hard at making them laugh, and ended up being a bear for them on the stone-flagged kitchen floor. Just before we left he produced, to my utter astonishment, two brown paper parcels from his pocket and I knew he must have stopped on the way to buy them himself: Mother's presents would have been with the big brightly-wrapped bundle upstairs.

We left Matthew racing a toy car around the kitchen and Ann with a small curly-haired black doll snug in her pinafore pocket. Colds and all, they rushed out into the icy farmyard to wave goodbye and I had never seen them so animated. I knew that if toys were given to them for birthdays or Christmas which were judged to be 'too good,' they were often taken away by my aunt to be donated elsewhere after the children had forgotten them.

'Curious,' my father mused as we drove away, ' a study for an anthropologist, that family.' Suddenly he braked, got out of the car when we were half way down the lane, and ran back towards my waving aunt. 'Compliments of the season to P. J.,' he shouted, and my aunt called genially, 'I'll tell him, Daniel. He's away out with a sick cow.' Impatiently I waited until my father returned and urged him to drive as fast as he could until that loathsome place was out of sight.

At home everything was beautiful. Even the brasses on the green hall door glittered as I'd never noticed before and a huge mass of red-berried holly was arranged in a brass pot-stand before the fresh white lace curtains. In the dark little hall there was more holly and ivy and then suddenly there was my mother rushing from her sewing-machine to scoop me up like a small boy into her arms. She smelled of *eau de cologne* and her brown hair newly-washed was breaking loose from its pins and she had apple cheeks. Not handsome, not young, but unlike her sister Ellen, wholesome and reassuring and – suddenly I saw it – happy.

And then the house. Never before I went to stay in the house that Ellen made had I noticed the touches that made ours different from the other houses in our modest terrace and a veritable palace in comparison with the O'Boyles' house. At the foot of the little staircase that glittered with old brass stair-rods was the grandfather clock of carved mahogany which my father had never been able to bring himself to sell. Its brass face shone, and its chime was as mellow as the polished wood. Gradually he pushed it into the background of his secondhand furniture shop until finally it had arrived here and would stay, as he told my mother, until somebody offered him what it was worth. Our equivalent of the O'Boyles' 'room', which was used by us always on Sundays and whenever anybody dropped in, had a red Turkish carpet that my father also claimed nobody had ever offered him a proper price for; it had a lot of old brasses too, and oddments of antique furniture kept in gleaming order by my mother who pretended to believe the fiction that any piece might at any time be sold for a fortune. She would have kept it gleaming anyway. Always in the centre of the round mahogany table was a bowl of flowers, or berries, or autumn leaves, always something fresh. Today there was more holly, and beside the hanging Chippendale wall-cabinet a little Christmas tree, the first we ever had. They were only beginning to be popular in Ireland when I was a child and naturally only the wealthy could afford them. As I exclaimed over the pretty thing, my mother bent down to put in the plug and the tree came alive with fairy lights and shimmering baubles.

Father attempted to heap more coal on the blazing fire, pausing to say over his shoulder to my mother: 'Are you sure now, Peg, you didn't let the sun at this fire earlier in the day? – it looks a bit dawny to me!'

And then all the news of Gurteenbeg came out, my mother laughing as she was expected to do over Ellen's theory about the sun's destructive rays. Wandering restlessly around the cosy room, I wanted to tell her about the full horrors of the place I had left, but I found it difficult.

She and my father regarded the O'Boyle marriage as something to be amused at and, certainly to be grateful for since they couldn't afford to send me to St John's College as a boarder. There was something slightly affectionate in their jeering which disturbed me. They didn't *know*.

Off and on during Christmas I tried to tell them. It was hopeless. I tried to tell them – especially my mother – how I hated Gurteenbeg and everybody in it except Bernie. I tried to tell her about the hunger and the cold that were part of accepted daily life there, about the gloom that settled over my head like a cloud as I approached the house from school every evening, about evil-smelling P. J. and the crimping meanness of Ellen. My mother turned the talk so neatly whenever I approached danger points that quite suddenly I realised she didn't want to know. She didn't want to know because boarding with the O'Boyles for the moderate sum agreed on was my only chance of a 'suitable' education, the sort neither she nor my father had been given, that would in due course lead to the university in Dublin and all they desired for me. My acceptance of the O'Boyle footbridge for what it was, they took for granted, and as Christmas ebbed away I began to grow desperate.

Once I even thought of describing to her what I had seen P. J. do to Bernie when he waylaid her one night on her way back from milking the cows, but I had no words for that extraordinary sight, only an obscure but positive feeling that my mother would refuse to understand even that. Especially that, because it would have been considered something I had no right to know if I had been minding my books and my own business.

And so came the day when we put away the Christmas baubles in cardboard boxes, as we did every year, and the fire was noisy with dry crackling holly. That was the day I made my last appeal.

'Don't send me back and I'll do anything for you.'

'Such as?' grinned my father.

'Such as studying night and day at home for my exam even if it kills me,' I said recklessly.

'In which case you wouldn't pass it,' said my father. 'Look, Dan, you know you *have* to go to school.'

'Can't you let me go back to the Christian Brothers, then?'

'Why not?' said my father happily, always less fiercely ambitious than my mother. 'Why not, Peg?'

But this was apparently too much. Dropping a box that had once held Christmas crackers and would now house the glass baubles which she had protected with tissue paper over the years, my mother flung herself into an armchair and wept noisily as my father and I swept the shattered spun glass off the carpet. Then I helped him wrap up again in their coloured tissues those baubles which had escaped the holocaust.

We put them away on the highest shelf of the china cupboard and I knew with a shrivelling of the soul that Christmas was over and that Gurteenbeg with its multiple miseries must be faced, as my father advised, like a man. And indeed in the clear cold challenge of January I knew too that I would never under any circumstances think like a child again.

CHRISTMAS WITH THE O'CONNORS

MAEVE BINCHY

Christmas Day, for Elizabeth, had always been an anticlimax; so much looked forward to, so much talked about, but when it came it always seemed to bring some disapproval, or some other cause for complaint which she would pretend not to notice. Last year it had been one long discussion about rationing and arguments about how they could possibly manage. Elizabeth thought that the Day with the O'Connors would be utterly perfect. She expected a story-book Christmas for the first time in her life.

For weeks they had all been making each other presents, and the cry of 'Don't come in!' arose whenever you went into a room unexpectedly. To Elizabeth's great surprise, Aisling talked enthusiastically about Santa Claus. Once or twice, Elizabeth had ventured a small doubt about him.

'Do you think that there actually might not be a Santa Claus, you know, the gifts might come from . . . somewhere else?'

'Don't be daft,' Aisling said. 'Sure, where else would they come from?' She had lit several candles asking God to remind Santa Claus of her requests.

Elizabeth had changed a great deal in her four months with the O'Connors. Once upon a time, she would have said nothing and just hoped that things would turn out for the best. Now, however, she felt able to intervene.

'Auntie Eileen?'

'Yes, darling?' Eileen was writing in the big household book she filled in every Saturday.

'I don't want to interfere but . . . you see, Aisling is praying to the Holy Family people in the church and asking them to tell Santa Claus that she wants a bicycle . . . and, you know . . . just . . . I thought you should know as well, if you see what I mean, just in cast she doesn't tell you.'

Eileen pulled the child towards her affectionately. 'Now, that's very kind of you to tell me that,' she said.

'It's not that I'm asking you to buy expensive things like that, it's just that Aisling believes very strongly that what you tell Santa Claus should be a secret, and she mightn't tell you.'

'Well, I'll keep that information very carefully in my mind,' said Eileen, solemnly. 'Run off with you, now.'

Christmas Eve was like a combination of Saturday nights with all the shoe polishing and neck washing, and the day of the Christmas play at school, all feverish excitement. Even grown-up people like Maureen and her friend Berna were giggling, and Young Sean was happy and wrapping up parcels.

During the night Elizabeth heard the door open. She glanced worriedly over at Aisling's bed but the red hair out on the pillow never stirred. Through half-closed eyes Elizabeth saw Sean place the bicycle, wrapped in brown paper and holly sprigs, at the end of Aisling's bed. And to her amazement she saw a similar shape coming to the end of her own bed. Two sharp trickles of tears began in her eyes. They were such a kind family, she would never be able to thank them. She must really try to explain to Mother in her next letter how kind they were.

Please could she find words that wouldn't irritate Mother and make Mother feel that she was being criticised.

Then it was morning and there were screams of excitement as Aisling in pyjamas tore off the wrapping paper. As Elizabeth swung her legs out of bed, Aisling, her face flushed with happiness, came over and gave her a great hug. She forced herself to put her arms around Aisling too. Though this was a new experience and she was always nervous of something new. Up to now they had only linked arms when coming home from school. That had been the closest contact. But now it was a sea of affection and excitement and it almost drowned Elizabeth with its unfamiliarity.

But in no time there were shouts and calls, and squeaks and hoots on a trumpet, and more shouts . . .

'Down here in two minutes or Christmas or no Christmas you'll feel the palm of my hand.'

It was still dark as they went up the hill to the church calling and wishing people Happy Christmas. Several people asked Elizabeth what she got in her stocking . . . and Doctor Lynch, Berna's father, pinched her cheek and asked her was an Irish Christmas better than an English one. His wife pulled him away crossly.

There were sausages and eggs for breakfast, paper table napkins on the table. Niamh sat up in her high chair and gurgled at them. There was more suppressed excitement since presents were going to be given afterwards beside the fire. The big things had come in the night but the individual ones would come now, and then the girls could go out in the square with their bicycles, Maureen could parade with her new jacket and matching beret, Eamonn with his football and boots, Donal with his scooter. Then it would be in again for the huge goose that was already cooking in the range.

There were oohs and aahs over the presents, the pincushions, the bookmarks, the dish painted as an ashtray for Da, the necklace made of carefully threaded beads. But there was the greatest applause for the presents that Maureen gave. For Mam there was beautiful soap, and for Da there was a proper man's scarf. For Aisling and Elizabeth big bangles with coloured glass in them; for Eamonn a big light for his bicycle; for Donal a funny furry hat, and even for the baby a rattle. She had given her elder brother two matching hair brushes like gentlemen used in picture books, and for Peggy she had a sparkling brooch.

Maureen had been the last to do the distributing. She asked if she could be and it seemed a glorious end to the present-giving. The air was so full of gratitude and re-examination of gifts that none of them except Elizabeth noted the anxious glances exchanged between Auntie Eileen and Uncle Sean. She couldn't interpret them – it was as if they alone had seen some hidden disaster. Uncle Sean evidently had decided to let Auntie Eileen deal with it, whatever it was. Elizabeth's face was reddening with anxiety, she knew it was.

'Right everyone, clear up all the mess, paper into this box, string into that, and *don't lose anything*!' Eileen supervised a huge sweep on the room. 'Now all of you out in the square, yes, you too, Sean, get a bit of exercise . . . and Donal, of course you can child . . . wrap up well. No, leave your furry hat here, that's the boy.'

In minutes she had the room cleared of people and presents. Elizabeth's heart pounded because she knew something was very wrong. She went into the kitchen with Peggy and helped to fold the paper up into squares. Peggy kept up a monologue about how much there was to be done for the meal and how little help anyone gave . . . but she was only muttering, and didn't expect any answer.

The voices came clearly from the next room.

'No, Maureen, sit down. Come on sit down . . . '

'I don't know what you mean Ma, what is it?'

'Maureen, where did you get the money to pay for these things . . . where?'

'Ma, I don't know what you mean. I saved up my pocket money like everyone else . . . of course I did Ma.'

'We're not fools Maureen . . . look at these things. They cost a fortune. That soap you bought your mother . . . it's fifteen shillings. I saw it myself in the chemist.'

'But Da, I didn't . . . '

'Just tell us where you got the money child, that's all your father and I want to know. Tell us quickly and don't ruin the day for all the rest of them.'

'I never took any of your money Mam, you can look in your desk, I didn't take a penny . . . '

'I didn't miss anything Sean.'

'And I didn't touch anything in your pocket, Da . . . '

'Come on, Maureen, you get a shilling a week, you have pounds worth of stuff here. Pounds and pounds. Can't you see your mother and I are heart-scalded over it . . . '

'Is this the thanks I get for giving you nice Christmas

23

presents . . . ' Maureen had begun to cry. 'Is this . . . all . . . you . . . say accuse me of stealing from you.'

'Well, the only other alternative . . . is that you stole from the shops.' Eileen's voice was shaking as she voiced the suspicion.

'I *bought* them,' persisted Maureen.

'God almighty, those hair brushes you gave Sean, they're over two pounds!' roared Sean. 'You're not leaving this room till we know. Christmas dinner or no Christmas dinner . . . if I have to shake every bone out of your body, I'll find out. Don't treat us like fools. *Bought* them indeed . . . '

'You'll have to tell us sooner or later, your father is right. Tell us now.'

'I bought you Christmas presents to please you and this is all you say . . . '

'I'm going to go up to Doctor Lynch's house and see whether their family got fine presents from that Berna of theirs. Maybe the two of you were in this together. Maybe Berna will tell us if you won't . . . '

'No!' it was a scream. 'No Da, don't go. Please don't go.'

There were sobs from Eileen, and shocked noises and wailings from Maureen as well as her mother. There was the sound of great slappings and a chair turning over. Elizabeth heard Aunt Eileen pleading with Uncle Sean not to be so hard.

'Leave her, Sean, leave her till you calm down.'

'Calm down. Stealing from every other trader in the town. Into their shops with that brat of a Lynch girl. Five shops, five families who've done business with us for years and this brat goes in and steals from them. Jesus Christ, what's there to be calm about . . . you're going in to every one of them when the shops open. Every single one of them do you hear, every item will be returned. And the Lynches will be told too, mind that. They're not going to live in innocence over the pair of thieves we have stalking the town . . . '

Elizabeth exchanged a fearful glance with Peggy as they heard another blow and another scream.

'Don't you be minding all that now,' said Peggy. 'Better not to poke your nose into others' affairs. Better to hear nothing and say nothing.'

'I know,' said Elizabeth. 'But it's going to spoil Christmas.'

'Not at all,' said Peggy. 'We'll have a grand Christmas.'

'Ah, Da you can't hit a girl like that, stop it, Da, stop it!'

'Go away, Sean, I don't want you here, get out, it's my business.'

'Da, you can't hit Maureen like that, Ma stop him, he's hit her on the head. Stop it, Da, stop it, you're too big, you'll kill her.'

Elizabeth fled from the kitchen and got her new bicycle. Round and round the square she cycled, trying to brush the tears out of her eyes. She didn't want the others to ask her what was wrong. She had no hope that they would even get together for the goose now. Aunt Eileen had probably gone to the bedroom, Sean gone off out after the row with his father. Uncle Sean might have taken the keys and gone back into the store, and Maureen – heaven knew what would happen to Maureen. It was all turning out badly like everything always did. It was so unfair.

From *Light a Penny Candle*

THE JOURNEY TO SOMEWHERE ELSE

ANNE DEVLIN

The snowroad to the Alps runs south-east from Lyons to Chambéry, whereafter, leaving the autoroute behind, it takes up with a steep mountain road north to Mégève on the western slopes of Mont Blanc.

The resort café, several miles above the village, was full of seventeen-year-old French millionaires – or so it seemed to us – and large Italian families: the women wore fur hats with their ski-suits and too many rings for comfort; their men had paunches and smoked cigars at lunch; and the twelve-year-old Italian girls confirmed for all time that fourteen was the only age to marry and Capulet's daughter might never have been such a catch had she lived long enough to look like her mother. There were probably some large French families as well, but they were less inclined to sit together as a group. The resort on the borders with Switzerland and Italy was fairly cosmopolitan; confirming too that the rich, like their money, are not different but indifferent to frontiers. Whatever nation they came from, they had nannies for their children, who cut up the food at different tables and did not ski. On Christmas Day opposite me a black woman peeled a small orange and fed it to a fat white child, piece by piece. The smell did it: satsumas!

Christmas Day in '59; they ran the buses in Belfast; the pungent smell of orange brought it back. My brother, the satsumas in green and red silver paper on the piano in the parlour, the fire dying in the grate and the adults asleep in their rooms. And that year, in '59 when I was eight, it had begun to snow. The grate-iron to rest the kettle on squeaked as I pushed it towards the coals with my foot.

'You'll burn your slipper soles,' Michael John said.

'I'm bored.'

'We could go out.'

'How?'

'The bus passes to the City Hall every fifteen minutes.'

'They'll not allow us. I've no money and – '

'Ah go on, Amee. I dare you,' he said. 'Run out, catch the next bus to the City Hall and come back up on it without paying.'

'But the conductor will put me off!'

'That's the dare. See how far you can get. The person who gets furthest wins!'

My brother was small and fair and mischievous; there was ten months difference in our ages.

'All right then, I'll go.'

Joe is dark and tall and mostly silent; there is ten years between us.

'Would you like me to get one for you?' Joe said, putting the lunch tray on the table in front of me. 'Amee, would you like one?'

'What?'

'The oranges you keep staring at,' he said, handing me a glass of cold red wine.

'I'm sorry. No. I don't really like them very much.'

'Your're shivering.'

'The wind's so cold.'

'Grumble. Grumble.'

'I'm sorry.'

With the life in the room the windows in the café clouded over.

'It would help if you stopped breathing,' he joked, as the window next to us misted.

It was a doomed journey from the start. Like all our holidays together it was full of incidents, mishaps and narrow escapes. Once, in Crete, I nearly drowned. I fell off his mother's boyfriend's boat and swallowed too much water. I remember coming up for air and watching him staring at me from the deck; he had been a lifesaver on a beach one summer, but I swam to those rocks myself. Four years ago in Switzerland, where he was working at the time, I fell on a glacier mountain, the Jungfrau, and slid headlong towards the edge with my skis behind me. I screamed for several minutes before I realised that if I continued to panic I would probably break my neck. I stopped screaming and thought about saving myself. At which point everything slowed down and I turned my body round on the snow, put my skis between me and the icy ridge and came to a halt. When I had enough energy I climbed back up. I suppose what happened this time was inevitable. About an hour after we crossed the Channel he crashed the car in Béthune. He drove at speed into the back of the one in front. I saw the crash coming and held my breath. On the passenger side we ended up minus a head-lamp and with a very crumpled wing.

'Why didn't you shout if you saw it coming?' he objected later.

'It seemed a waste of energy,' I said. 'I couldn't have prevented it happening.'

We exchanged it for a French car at Arrais and after I travelled apprehensively towards the Alps.

'Why don't we ski separately?' I suggested, after the first week. 'I'd like some ski lessons. Anyway, you're a far more advanced skier. I only hold you back.'

On the second day of that week I came back from ski class at four thirty and waited for him in the café by the main telecabin. There were so few people inside now the glass was almost clear. A family group sat at one table and ski instructors at the bar drank cognac. I waited for half an hour before I noticed the time.

It was snowing heavily outside then as well, and even getting dark. The snow was turning blue in the light. I closed the heavy front door behind me lightly till the snib caught and ran across the road to wait at the stop. I could see him watching at the lace curtains in the sitting room. The Christmas-tree lights were on in the room, the curtain shifted. Soundlessly, the bus arrived. I got on, and just as quietly it moved off. The conductor was not on the platform, nor was he on the lower deck, so I went to the front and crouched low on the seat and hoped he wouldn't notice me when he did appear. There was no one else aboard but two old ladies in hats with shopping baskets and empty Lucozade bottles. Noisily, the conductor came downstairs. He stood on the platform clinking small change; I could see his reflection in the glass window of the driver's seat. If I was lucky he would not bother me, I was too far away from the platform. Suddenly, he started to walk up the bus. I looked steadfastly out of the window. He rapped the glass pane to the driver and said something. The driver nodded. He spoke again. I was in such terror of a confrontation that I didn't hear anything he said. For a moment he glanced in my direction, and he remained where he stood. We were nearing the cinemas at the end of the road. At this point I decided not to go all the way round the route to the City Hall. I got up quickly and walked down the bus away from him and stood uneasily on the platform. At the traffic lights before the proper stop, he moved along the bus towards me, my nerve failed and I leaped off.

'Hey!' he called out. 'You can't get off here.'

It was snowing more heavily. Wet snow. My feet were cold. I looked down and saw that I was still wearing my slippers; red felt slippers with a pink fur trim. How strange I must have looked in a duffel coat and slippers in the snow. The clock of the Presbyterian Assembly Buildings read five forty-five. It chimed on the quarter-hour, and behind me the lights of a closed-up confectioner's illuminated a man I had not noticed before. 'You'll get your nice slippers wet,' he said.

'I'll dry them when I get home,' I said.

'You'll get chilblains that way.'

'No I won't.'

I looked doubtfully at my slippers; the red at the toes was darker than the rest and my feet felt very uncomfortable.

'Have you far to walk when you get off the bus?' he asked.

'No. I live just up the road. The bus passes my house,' I said.

'You'd better stand in here. It's drier,' he said.

'I didn't answer. At that moment a young woman came round the corner into view and began walking towards us from the town centre. She walked with difficulty through the snow in high shoes. Under her coat a black dress and white apron showed as she moved. The woman looked at me and then at the man and stopped. She drew a packet of cigarettes from her apron pocket and lit one. At first she waited at the stop with me, and then, shivering, moved back into the protective shelter of the shop by the man's side.

'That wind 'ud go clean through you so it would,' she said.

'Aye. It comes in off the Lough and goes straight up the Black Mountain,' he said, looking away up the road. The woman and I followed his gaze.

Beyond us, a block or two away, was the dolls' hospital, we had been there a few weeks before with my mother.

'Leave the aeroplanes alone, Michael John,' she scolded. 'Just wait and see what Santa brings you.'

I loved that shop with all its dolls, repaired, redressed. My own doll had started out from there as a crinoline lady in white net with hoops and red velvet bows. That year, when we left it at the shop minus a leg, it had been returned to me as a Spanish dancer in a petticoat of multicoloured layers. We only ever visited the town with my mother; during the day when it was busy and friendly, when the matinées at the cinema were going in and traffic moved around the centre, the cinema confectioner's shop in front of which I stood was always open and sold rainbow drops and white chocolate mice – the latter turned up in my stocking – so were there too, I noticed for the first time, satsumas in that window.

The snow, and the quiet and the darkness had transformed the town. In the blue-grey light the charm of the life went out of it, it seemed unfamiliar, dead. I wanted to go home to the fire in the parlour; I began to shiver convulsively, and then the bus came.

'Ardoyne.' The woman looked out. 'That's my bus.'

I was so grateful I forgot about the dare.

'No good to you?' she said to the man.

He shook his head and pulled up the collar of his coat.

'Merry Christmas,' she called out as we got on.

I was sitting brazenly at the seat next to the platform when the conductor turned to me for the fare.

'I forgot my purse,' I said. 'But this bus passes my house, my Mammy'll pay for it when I get home.'

'Oh, your Mammy'll pay it when you get home!' he mimicked. 'Did you hear that now!'

The young woman, who had gone a little further up the bus, turned round. We had only moved a couple of streets beyond the stop, the toyshop was behind me. A wire cage encased its shop front.

'Please don't put me off now,' I said, beginning to cry.

'I'll pay her fare,' the young woman said.

'Does your Mammy know you're out at all?' he asked and, getting no answer, moved along to the woman. 'Where are you going to anyway?' he called back.

'The stop before the hospital stop,' I said weakly.

'The Royal,' he said to the woman. The ticket machine rolled once.

'And Ardoyne. The terminus,' she said.

The ticket machine rolled once and they grumbled between them about having to work on Christmas Day.

'I'll be late getting my dinner tonight. Our ones'll all have finished when I get in.'

'Aye, sure I know. I'm not off till eight,' he said. 'It's hardly been worth it. The one day in the year.' He snapped the tickets off the roll and gave her change. 'And no overtime.'

Someone, a man, clambered downstairs to the platform. He had a metal tin under his arm. The conductor pulled the bell.

'No overtime?' You're kiddin', she said.

'That's the Corporation for you,' he said.

Before the hospital stop he pulled the bell again. I stepped down to the platform. I could see the Christmas-tree lights in the bay window of the parlour. I jumped off and ran towards the house, and wished I hadn't been too ashamed to thank her. But her head was down and she wasn't looking after me.

Michael John opened the door. 'You did it?' he said, half in awe. 'I saw you get off the bus. You did it!'

'Yes,' I gasped. My heart was pounding and my feet hurt.

'All the way to the City Hall?'

'Of course.'

He followed me into the parlour.

'But look at your slippers, Amee, they're ruined. You went out in your slippers. They'll know.'

'Not if I dry them. No one will ever know.'

I put my slippers on the fender and stood looking at the red dye on the toes of my white tights. I pulled off the stockings as well and saw that even my toes were stained.

'Look at that, Michael John! My toes are dyed!' I said. 'Michael John?'

The front door closed so quietly it was hardly audible.

'Michael John! Don't go!'

From the sitting-room window I could see him crossing the road.

'Oh, I only pretended,' I breathed. 'I didn't.'

But he was too far away. And then the bus came.

I waited at that window until my breathing clouded the glass. I rubbed it away with my fist. Every now and then I checked the slippers drying at the fender. Gradually the dark red faded, the toes curled up and only a thin white line remained. I went back to the window and listened for the bus returning. Several buses did come by, but Michael John did not. I got under the velvet drapes and the lace and stood watching at the glass where the cold is trapped and waited. I could tell him the truth when he came back. The overhead lights of the sitting room blazed on and my mother's voice called:

'Ameldia! What are you doing there?'

She looked crossly round the room.

'You've let the fire go out! Where is Michael John?'

'Excusez-moi? Madame Fitzgerald?' the waitress in the café asked.

34

My ski pass lay on the table, she glanced at it briefly; the photograph and the name reassured her.

'Telephone!' she said, indicating that I should follow.

The ski instructors at the bar turned their heads to watch as I passed by to the phone. They were the only group left in the café. I expected to hear Joe's voice, instead a woman at the other end of the line spoke rapid French.

'Please. Could you speak English?' I asked.

She repeated her message.

'Your friend is here at the clinic in the village. We have X-rayed him. He will now return to your hotel. Can you please make your own way back.'

'Yes. But what is wrong?'

'I'm, sorry?'

'What is wrong with him?'

'An accident. Not serious.'

'Thank you, I said, and hurried away from the phone.

Outside it was dark and still snowing. I knew two routes back to the village: there was the mountain route we had skied down on after class a few days before, half an hour earlier by the light; and there was the route by road which we had driven up on in the morning. I could also take the bus. It was five twenty. The lifts and telecabins closed nearly an hour before. The bus which met the end of ski class had long gone; so too had the skiers to the town. The only people left seemed to be resort staff and instructors, most of whom lived on the mountain. It took five minutes to ski down to the village on the mountain, and forty-five minutes to go by road – if a bus came. Without further hesitation I made the decision to take the shortest route back. It was too dark to ski, so I put my skis on my shoulder and started out to walk along the ski-track down the mountain.

I followed the path confidently at first, encouraged by the sight of three young men who were walking fairly swiftly ahead. Half-way down the hill through a farm, which even in deep snow smelt of farming, I passed a woman going in the opposite direction, who looked at me briefly and said:

'Bonsoir, madame.'

The surprise in her voice and the weight of the skis on my shoulder arrested me momentarily so I stopped: 'Bonsoir.'

I shifted my skis to my other shoulder and in so doing realised that I had lost sight of the other walkers ahead. I walked on to a turning point by a chalet and found there that the path forked two ways. There was no one ahead any more, and looking back uphill I found that the woman had disappeared. The lights of the village twinkled before me, directly below the treeline, luring me down the slope. The other path stretched more gradually down around the mountain. In the light it had been so easy. I stood for a moment staring at the mute grey wetness. Were there really two tracks? The longer I stood in the dark looking, the more confusing it became. If I don't move now it will be too late. I moved. I set off again rapidly downhill, but the weight of the skis on my shoulder and the slippery gradient propelled me onwards at a hair-raising speed towards the treeline. The hard plastic boots made it impossible to grip the snow. I slipped badly and then stopped suddenly against the slope. My legs shook. I was breathless. If I moved another inch I would probably break a leg. Lost. I'm lost as well. If I could only be sure that this was the right way. Perhaps the wider, more gradual path is the one. I set off to climb back to the fork again. A light in the chalet further up the slope reassured me. I could always ask there.

Breathless, I regained the beginning of the two paths. I did not approach the chalet, but set out confidently on the wider path. The route ran between the snowdrifts higher on the mountain side than on the valley, but I saw also that now I was leaving the lights of the village behind, and this path, although easier to follow, was leading directly into a wood of pines above me. I came to a small grotto on the valley side of the slope, and beyond, a little further up the mountain, I could see the white stone façade of a closed church. A mound of snow nestling uneasily on the steep roof of the grotto slid off quietly in slow motion into my path, seconds before I reached it. Perversely, I blundered on. This is the wrong way, I'm sure it is, I thought. More precious energy sapped by the extra effort of wading through the drift, I came once more to a halt. The wind blew relentlessly. I noticed it for the first time. There is something noxious about the innocence of snow in its insidious transformation of familiar routes. I must go back. I turned and hurried back between the church and grotto, and reached, with a great deal of effort, the turning point on the path yet again. If I meet someone now, will they be friend or foe? If I go to that chalet to ask, will I be welcome? If I could somehow find the energy to climb further. I suddenly understood more perfectly than at any other moment that Fate, like a love affair, is a matter of timing: the right person passing at the right time; a combination of moments from experience which keep coming round like a memory, recurring, inducing in us the same confusion. It was as though I had stood all my life in the same cold place between the curtain and the glass. How stupid I am. This whole journey is pointless, I said aloud to no one, I could have gone for the bus. I closed my eyes and breathed painfully.

'Where is Michael John, Ameldia? Why did you let him go? You're older, you should be more responsible! What bus? At what time?'

The conductor remembered him. He didn't have any money. No, he didn't put him off. On Christmas Day for thrupence? It wasn't worth it. He didn't remember when he got off. He hadn't seen him get off. There was a memorial service on the feast of the Purification; they waited and waited. There was no coffin, only flowers in the church, and my mother's tears all during the service. He went away so completely, he even went out of my dreams. Fair and small and mischievous.

When I opened my eyes a white mist was forming. I would have to hurry and get to the road before it enveloped me completely. Every step uphill was excruciatingly painful as again and again the skis bit into my shoulder. As I neared the top of the hill, passing through the farm smells, I heard voices. Two girls and a boy appeared, I went slowly, passing them higher up the slope; I had climbed very high. They took the downward path, several feet of snow separated us. They did not glance in my direction and I had lost my curiosity about the route. We passed in silence. I got to the road again where I started out exhausted. Did anyone pass him that night and not know?

Once on the highway I walked more easily where the traffic of the day had beaten down the snowtrack. My alarm had evaporated like the mist on the mountain. But I was hungry and tired and when I reached the car-park where the ski bus turned it was deserted, no one was waiting. I put the skis into a bank of snow and lay against them. My face burned, and my hair clung to my forehead from the effort and panic of climbing. A car passed. It was too dark to read my watch. If I walked on to the road towards the lights I would be able to read the time. I was too tired to move. My shoulders ached. I could not lift my arms above my head. My clothes clung. The backs of my knees were damp. My leather gloves looked swollen and bloated. Another car passed. It must be late; perhaps he will come out looking for me. If I go and stand on the road he might see me. I was too weary to move, so I stayed on. Then a familiar throaty rattle of an engine sounded, and a bus turned into the coach-park.

'Mégève?'

'Non, Sallandes.'

'Oh,' I must have looked disappointed.

'Dix minutes!' he assured me.

'Oh. Merci, monsieur!' I brightened.

He was back in half the time to pick me up. I dropped my skis into the cage at the back and in a few minutes we were hurtling down the mountain towards the village.

At seven thirty I got to the hotel. Joe was not there. The X-rays from the clinic were lying on the bed. Perhaps he was worried and has gone out looking for me, I thought. I was drying my wet clothes on the radiators when he came in.

'What on earth happened?' I asked at the sight of the sling.

'Oh, some idiot got out of control and jumped on my back this afternoon. Arrogant lout. He didn't even apologise. He said I shouldn't have stopped suddenly in front of him.'

'Why did you stop?'

'A girl in front of me fell down. I stopped to help her.'

'It's dangerous though, isn't it? You should have skied round her to safety and then stopped.'

'Well, anyway, I won't be able to ski again this holiday,' he said. 'The ligaments are torn.'

'Is is very painful?'

'It's a bit sore.'

'I'm sorry. Shall we go back tomorrow?'

'Well, we could go to Paris tomorrow instead of on Friday.'

'Let's do that, I'll drive,' I said.

'There's no need. I can manage. I have no trouble driving,' he said. 'How are you then, all right? Had a nice day?'

'Joe, I got lost on the mountain.'

'Did you?' he said. 'Oh, by the way, I've been downstairs talking to Madame. I told here that we were leaving earlier. She was very sympathetic when she saw the sling. She said she wouldn't charge us for the extra nights even though we've booked to stay till Friday.'

'I tried to walk down the path we skied on and then I couldn't find it.'

'That was silly,' he said. 'Why didn't you get the bus?'

'I don't know.'

It wasn't the first time in our ten-year relationship of living together and not living together that I found I had nothing to tell him. He never guessed the fury of my drama; and now he looked pale and tired.

'What's the matter?' he asked, catching me watching him.

'Nothing. Nothing's the matter.'

Even in Montmartre there was snow and coldness.

'There's a hotel! Stop now!' I said.

We had been driving all day, yet it seemed as though we never left the snowline.

'Stop! Please. That hotel looked nice. Joe, I'm not navigating a street further.'

'Ameldia, it's a five-star hotel!' he said, in a voice that reminded me of my mother. 'We are not staying in a five-star hotel!'

'It's on me,' I said extravagantly. 'Whatever this costs, it's on me!'

'But Amee, you don't have any money!'

'I'll argue with the bank manager about that, not with you,' I said. 'I have a little plastic card here which will settle everything. Now, will you get out of the car? Please, Joe. you look exhausted!'

We signed into a fourth-floor side room. Through the nylon curtains I could see the traffic of Paris and the lights of the Eiffel Tower. 'We can walk to the Sacré Coeur from here. I think I remember the way,' I said.

My last visit had been as a schoolgirl fifteen years before.

There were tangerines in the restaurant – I lifted my head to them as they passed on the fruit tray to the table next to us

– and ice-cubes on the grapes. I shivered involuntarily. I don't remember satsumas any other year.

'I forgot to ring my mother on Christmas Day!' I said suddenly.

'From the French Alps? Why would you want to do that? he said.

'You know what they're like about me being away for Christmas.'

'No, I'm afraid I don't, I've never met them,' he said firmly.

'And I'm afraid I don't see why you think they should still be so obsessed with you. You are thirty years of age now, Ameldia, and you do have other brothers and sisters!'

'Yes, I know. But I was the only one around when – '

'Forget it!' he said. 'I didn't spend all this money and bring you all this way for you to drag that up now!'

'Madame? Monsieur?' A waiter stood eyeing us, his pencil poised like a dagger ready to attack his notepad.

Later as we passed through the square in Monmartre, sad-eyed artists were putting their easels away. An African spread out ivory bangles and elephants on a cloth on the pavement and I stopped to admire. He spoke English: 'Are you English?'

'No. Irlande.'

'Ah. Irlande is good,' he said, putting an arm around me and drawing me towards his wares. I felt like a schoolgirl again, shy, drawing away, explaining I had no money to buy anything. Joe watched me from a distance and I said: 'Don't me so grumpy.

'I'm not grumpy,' he said crossly.

'Wouldn't it be nice to go and have a glass of wine in one

of those bars,' I said.

'Well, they look very crowded to me and I'm tired,' he said.

'Do you know why I love Montmartre?'

'No, but I'm sure you're going to tell me!' he said.

'Because whatever time you come here, it's always open, full of people.'

I wished I hadn't brought him to Montmartre. He seemed so uneasy amidst the haggle of trading in the streets. I had forgotten how he hated markets. He did not relax until we got back to the hotel.

I was not tired and didn't find that sleep came easily. My tossing and turning kept him awake.

'Where did you get that cough from?' he asked.

'I must have got a cold somewhere.'

I got up and went to the fridge for a glass of mineral water, and as I opened the door in the dark, I thought I smelt oranges.

'Did you spill the fruit juice?' I asked.

''No,' he said wearily. 'When will you go to sleep?'

I went to the shower room to drink the water so as not to disturb him, and when I returned to the bedroom I found it was very much colder than when I'd left it. The curtain shifting slightly caught my attention. The glass in the window was so clear it looked as if it wasn't there at all.

'Joe?' I called softly. 'Did you open the window?'

'No,' he said without stirring.

The room appeared to be filling with a white mist. It's like on the mountain, I thought. The white mist of the night outside seemed to grow in the room.

'That's funny.' The smell of oranges was very strong.

'Somebody is eating satsumas!' I said aloud.

Joe didn't answer. I got into bed and lay down trembling. The walls of the room were gradually slipping away to the mist. 'No. I will not watch,' I said firmly. 'I will not watch any more.' I closed my eyes tight against the dark and breathed softly.

Where the white rocks of the Antrim Plateau meet the mud banks of the Lough, three small boys netting crabs dislodged a large stone, when one of them reaching into the water after the escaping crab caught instead the cold hand of my brother. In May, a closed coffin filled the sitting room and the Children of Mary from the neighbourhood came to pray there and keep the vigil.

'I will not watch,' I said. 'I will not watch.'

An angel of Portland stone marked the grave and we sang: 'Blood of my Saviour wash me in thy tide'. 'He was bound for heaven,' my mother said often, and that seemed to console her. And every Sunday of the year we went to the cemetery, my mother and I; on Christmas Day ever after we left offerings of flowers and things until even the angelstone aged, became pockmarked and turned brown. It was the first Christmas I had not gone to that grave.

In the morning Joe drew back the curtains in the room and said: 'What a sight! I'm glad I didn't know that was there last night.'

'Didn't know what?' I said, moving to the window.

'Look!'

A huddle of stone crucifixes, headstones and vaults marked the graves which jostled for the space under our window against the side wall of the hotel.

'Montmartre cemetery!' he said.

There were no angels among the headstones.

'How creepy! Well, I'm glad we're going,' he said, with a last glance before dropping the curtain.

But I could still see.

'Last night,' I began to say, 'this room was very cold and I asked you if – '

'Oh, do come away from that window and hurry up and pack,' he said. 'We need to catch the lunch-time ferry.'

I wanted to tell him what I now knew, that the future was already a part of what I was becoming, and if I stopped this becoming there would be no future, only an endless repetition of moments from the past which I will be compelled to relive. 'It would help if you stopped breathing,' he had said. But it wouldn't; because there would always be the memory of existence – like a snare; a trapped moment, hungover in the wrong time. Unaccountable. And I wanted to tell him before it was too late that the difference is as fragile between the living and the dead as the absence of breath on a glass. But already he was rushing on a journey to somewhere else.

Bound for heaven, was it? Yes. Hand and foot.

LAST BUS FOR CHRISTMAS

PATRICIA LYNCH

'Hurry up there, Miheal! Will ye bring over two red candles quick!'

'More strawberry jam, Miheal! Two one-pound jars! And raisins: four one-pound bags!'

'Miheal Daly! I'm wore out wid waitin' for twine. How can I parcel the customers' groceries wid ne'er an inch of string?'

Miheal grabbed a handful of string from the box in the corner behind the biscuit tins and ran with it to Mr Coughlan. He brought the jam and the raisins at the same time to Peter Cadogan, and rolled the candles along the counter to Jim Reardon. Then he went back to his job of filling half-pound bags with sugar.

Miheal was shop-boy and, one day, if he worked hard and behaved himself, Mr Coughlan had promised to make him an assistant.

'There's grandeur for an orphan!' Mrs Coughlan told him. 'Ye should be grateful.'

Miheal was grateful. But, as he watched the women crowding the other side of the counter, filling market bags and baskets with Christmas shopping, he was discontented. Yet he had whistled and sung as he put up the coloured paper chains and decorated the window with yards of tinsel and artificial holly.

He nibbled a raisin and gazed out at the sleet drifting past the open door.

Everybody's going home for Christmas but me, he thought.

The Coughlans always went to their relations for Christmas. Mrs Coughlan left Miheal plenty to eat and Mr Coughlan gave him a shilling to spend. But Miheal never ate his Christmas dinner until they came back. After Mass he spent Christmas Day walking about the streets, listening to the noise and clatter that came from the houses.

'Only two more hours,' whispered Peter Cadogan, as Miheal brought him bags of biscuits and half-pounds of rashers as fast as Mr Coughlan could cut them.

'Two more sugars, Miheal,' said Jim Reardon. 'Where d'you get your bus?'

Jim was new. He didn't know Miheal was an orphan, and Miheal was ashamed to tell him he had no home to go to for Christmas.

'Aston's Quay,' he muttered.

'We'll go together,' said Jim over his shoulder. 'I've me bag under the counter. Get yours!'

The next time Miheal brought Jim candles and raisins the new assistant wanted to know what time Miheal's bus went.

'I'll just make it if I run,' said Miheal.

'Then get yer bag, lad. Get yer bag!'

Miheal slipped through the door leading to the house. He ran to his little dark room under the stairs. He didn't dare switch on the light. Mrs Coughlan would want to know what he was doing. And a nice fool he'd look if she found out he was pretending to go home for Christmas.

'Home!' said Miheal to himself. 'That's where a lad's people come from and mine came from Carrigasheen.'

47

He wrapped his few belongings in an old waterproof. He grabbed his overcoat from the hook behind the door and was back in the shop before Mr Coughlan could miss him.

'Hi, Miheal! Give me a hand with this side of bacon. I never cut so many rashers in me life!'

Miheal pushed his bundle under the counter and ran to help.

'Isn't it grand to be going home for Christmas!' cried Peter, as they closed the door to prevent any more customers from coming in.

'Isn't it terrible to be turning money away!' groaned Mr Coughlan.

But Mrs Coughlan was waiting for him in her best hat and the coat with the fur collar.

'Can I trust you lads to bolt the shop door an' let yerselves out be the side door?' demanded Mr Coughlan.

'Indeed you can, sir!' replied Peter and Jim.

The last customer was served.

'I'm off!' cried Peter.

'Safe home!' called the others.

Then Jim was running down the quay, Miheal stumbling after him, clasping his bundle, his unbuttoned coat flapping in the wind.

They went along Burgh Quay, pushing by the people waiting for the Bray bus, then across to Aston's Quay.

'There's me bus!' shouted Jim.

"Tis packed full!' murmured Miheal. He was terribly sorry for Jim. But maybe he'd come back with him and they could spend Christmas together.

The bus was moving.

Jim gave a leap, the conductor caught his arm and pulled him to safety. He turned and waved to Miheal, his round red face laughing. He would have to stand all the way, but Jim was used to standing.

Two queues still waited. Miheal joined the longest.

'Where are ye bound for, avic?' asked a stout country-woman, with a thin little girl and four large bundles, who came up after him.

'Carrigasheen!' replied Miheal proudly.

'Ah, well! I never heard tell of the place. But no doubt ye'll be welcome when ye get there. An' here's the bus.'

'I'll help with the bundles, ma'am,' said Miheal politely.

Now every seat was filled. Still more people squeezed into the bus. Miheal reached the step.

'One more, an' one more only!' announced the conductor. 'In ye go, ma'am!' said Miheal, stepping back.

The little girl was in. Miheal pushed the bundles after her and everyone cried out when the conductor tried to keep back the stout woman.

'Sure ye can't take the child away from her mammy!' declared a thin man. 'Haven't ye any Christianity in yer bones?'

'Can't she sit on me lap?' demanded the stout woman. 'Give me a h'ist up, lad. And God reward ye!' she added, turning to Miheal.

He seized her under the arms. She caught the shining rail and Miheal gave a great heave.

He stood gazing after the bus.

'Now, I'm stranded!' he said, forgetting he had no need to

leave Dublin.

A dash of sleet in Miheal's face reminded him. He could go back to the lonely house behind the shop. His supper would be waiting on the table in the kitchen. He could poke up the fire and read his library book.

The quays were deserted. A tall garda strolled along. He stared curiously at Miheal and his bundle.

'Missed the bus, lad?' he asked.

''Twas full up,' explained Miheal.

'Bad luck!' sympathised the garda. 'Can ye go back where ye came from?'

Miheal nodded.

''Tis a bad night to be travelling!' said the garda. 'That's the way to look at it.'

He gave Miheal a friendly nod and passed on.

I'd as well be getting me supper, thought Miheal.

But he did not move.

Over the Metal Bridge came a queer old coach drawn by two horses. The driver was wrapped in a huge coat with many capes and a broad-brimmed hat was pulled down over his twinkling eyes.

He flourished a whip and pulled up beside Miheal.

The boy edged away. He didn't like the look of the coach at all.

The driver leaned over and managed to open the door at the back with his whip.

'In ye get! Last bus for Christmas!'

Whoever saw a bus with horses! thought Miheal. But I suppose they use any old traps at Christmas.

Still he held back.

'All the way to Carrigasheen widout stoppin!' said the driver.

Miheal could see the cushioned seats and the floor spread thick with fresh hay. The wind, which was growing fiercer and colder every moment, blew in his face. He gave one look along the desolate quay and, putting his foot on the iron step, scrambled in.

At once the door slammed shut. The driver gave a shout and the horses trotted over the stones.

The coach bumped and swayed. Miheal tried to stretch out on the seat, but he slipped to the floor. The hay was thick and clean. He put his bundle under his head for a pillow and fell asleep.

An extra bump woke him up.

'I never thought to ask the fare,' said Miheal to himself. 'Seems a long way, so it does. Would he want ten shillings? He might – easy! Well, I haven't ten shillings. I've two new half-crowns. He'll get one and not a penny more!'

He tried to stand up, the coach was swaying from side to side and he had to sit down again.

'Mister! Mister!' he shouted. 'How much is the fare?'

The rattling of the coach and the thunder of the horses' hooves made so much noise he could scarcely hear himself. Yet he would not keep quiet.

'I won't pay a penny more than two and six,' he shouted. 'Mind now! I'm telling you.'

The door of the coach swung open and Miheal was pitched out, his bundle following him. He landed on a bank covered with snow and lay there blinking.

The road wound away through the mountains in the moon-light – an empty desolate road. The wind had dropped but snow was falling.

In the distance he could hear a strange sound. It was coming nearer and nearer, and soon Miheal knew it was someone singing 'Adeste Fideles' in a queer cracked voice.

The singer approached, tramping slowly along: an old man with a heavy sack on his back.

'What ails ye to be sitting there in the snow, at this late hour of the night, young lad?' he asked, letting his sack slip to the ground.

'I came on the coach from Dublin,' replied Miheal, standing up.

He was ashamed to say he had fallen out.

The old man pushed back his battered caubeen and scratched his head.

'But there hasn't been a coach on this road in mortal memory!' he declared. 'There's the bus road the other side of the mountain and the last bus went by nigh on two hours ago. I suppose ye came by that. Where are ye bound for?'

'Mebbe I did come by the bus and mebbe I didn't!' exclaimed Miheal. 'But I'd be thankful if you'd tell me am I right for Carrigasheen?'

The old man wasn't a bit annoyed by Miheal's crossness.

'D'ye see the clump of trees where the road bends round by the mountain. There's Carrigasheen! I'm on me way there an' I'll be real glad of company. So ye're home for Christmas? I thought I knew everyone for miles around, yet I don't remember yer face. What name is on ye, lad?'

'Miheal Daly.'

The old man stared.

'There are no Dalys in Carrigasheen now. That I do know! But we can talk as we go. Me own name is Paudeen Caffrey.'

Miheal caught up the sack. He was a strong lad but he found it heavy. He wondered how the old man had managed to carry it at all. Paudeen Caffrey took the boy's bundle and they set off. The snow piled on their shoulders, on the loads they carried, on their hair, their eyebrows, but they did not notice, for Miheal was telling the old man all about himself.

'So me poor gossoon, ye're an orphan,' asked the old man.

'I am indeed!' agreed Miheal.

'An' ye haven't a father or mother, or brother or sister to be a friend to ye?'

'Not a soul!'

'An' these people ye work for, what class of people are they?' continued old Paudeen Caffrey.

'Not too bad!' declared Miheal. 'Aren't they going to make me an assistant one of these days?'

'Suppose now,' began the old man. 'Mind, I'm just saying suppose – ye have a chance to be shop-boy to an old man and his wife that needed help bad in their shop and couldn't get it? Mind ye – I'm only supposing. Ye'd have a room wid two windas, one lookin' out on the market square, the other at the mountains. Ye'd have three good meals a day, a snack at supper, ten shillings a week, an' if ye wanted to keep a dog or a cat, or a bicycle, ye'd be welcome. What would ye say to that?'

He looked at Miheal sideways and Miheal looked back.

'It wouldn't be with Paudeen Caffrey, that kept the corner

shop next the post office, would it? asked Miheal.

'It would so,' replied the old man.

'I'm remembering now,' said the boy. 'Me father told me if ever I needed a friend to write to Paudeen Caffrey.'

'Why didn't ye, lad? Why didn't ye?'

'I was ashamed. Me mother told me how they left Carrigasheen after telling everyone they were going to Dublin to make their fortunes an', when they came back, they'd be riding in their carriage. Ye see?'

The old man laughed.

'An' didn't ye come back in a carriage? But there's the lights of Carrigasheen. Do ye come home wid me, Miheal Daly?'

'If you'll have me, Mr Caffrey.'

'The old man chuckled.

'An' to think I went out for a sack of praties an' come back wid a shop-boy! Wasn't it well ye caught the last bus for Christmas, Miheal?'

'It was indeed!' declared Miheal Daly.

He could see the corner shop with the door open and an old woman looking out. Beyond her he caught a glimpse of firelight dancing on the walls, of holy pictures framed in holly and a big red Christmas candle on the table waiting for the youngest in the house to light it.

BUTTERFLY CHRISTMAS

TERRY PRONE

He had marched the Christmas trees out to where she sat in the car. Two by two, thumping their stumps into the pavement and twirling them. The first two she rejected.

'Spacer,' she said decidedly, then shook her head as a wet dog does, the two rigid hands rising off her lap to sketch in the air.

'Spacer,' she said again, helplessly.

A couple of passers-by, one clutching two turkeys by the neck in much the same way as her husband held the trees, stopped to watch.

'Bigger around?' her husband asked. She was silent.

'Taller?'

The nod was frantic.

'No problem,' he said, and marched the shorter trees away.

The chosen tree was now anchored in a clever red contraption that held water, and five sets of tiny lights had been threaded all over it. Today, he would put up the decorations. She went to turn in the bed and failed. The reflexes of mobility don't give up easily, she reflected. Nor the dreams, filled with unplanned, unquestioned movement.

'Very fortunate your ribs weren't broken,' he said, sliding out his side of the bed and heading for the bathroom. 'You'd never have managed without the deep sighs.'

Snorting laughter overcame her, alone in the big bed. The

snorts had been there since childhood, but in self-conscious adolescence she had developed the habit of cupping a hand over mouth and nose so that her laughter made a drowned noise. Now, neither hand could reach mouth and nose. Thinking about this provoked an itch beside her nostril. She concentrated on it, having been taught that if you tried to make it get worse, rather than better, you could eventually make it go away, because your brain lost interest in paying so much attention to one small irritant. The itch stayed and worsened, unaware of the sophisticated psychology being applied to it. It took ownership of her as pain never had. In the intensive care unit, staff had driven her berserk by their solicitude for the pain. Pain control was now in fashion. Everybody was geared to stop it before it started, as opposed to the old days, when it was allowed to become a raging torrent before the easing needle was employed. Nobody, however, was geared to take an itch seriously, and for her, the itches were worse than pain.

He was beside her with a rough dry face cloth. It was rubbed impersonally all over her face, scouring the itch away. The cloth then went into the bowl of hot water he had carried in, its coarse terry loops softening so that when he washed her face, it was a warm wet infusion of comfort.

'This is gonna hurt you more than it hurts me,' he said, as he now always did, before cleaning her teeth.

The jaws were locked, leaving only an inch of access. The brush, scrubbing against the enamel, was loud in her ears as he talked to her, the words lost. She looked a question at him, but he seemed contented with her lack of response, and dressed her, buttoning her blouse right up to the collar as if readying her in a school uniform.

'I've solved the problem of getting you downstairs,' he said, looping one of her arms over his shoulder and lifting her. As he carried her across the small landing, she could feel the redness rising in her face for shame at her own heaviness.

'Now, I'm going to lean you against the wall and slide you down,' he said, ignoring her anxious grunts.

The painted wall was smooth and chill against the white blouse as he slid her down into a sitting position at the top of the stairs, where he had laid the single bed duvet. Once she was seated, he pulled the plaster rigidities of her legs out in front of her, pointing down the stairs towards where he was, a few steps below her. He then tipped her forward, so that her head was on his shoulder, and gently pulled the duvet, so that her bottom went bump from one step to another, her forehead hitting the soft padded shoulder of his cardigan in an off-tempo echo. She began to laugh at the awkward efficiency of it, sucking in hairs from the cardigan at every in-breath.

Three steps from the bottom he straightened her up as briskly as if she had been a shop mannequin, and hefted her into the wheelchair.

'*Now*,' he said, kicking off the brake of the wheelchair with enormous satisfaction. 'Now.'

He parked her where she could watch the flames of the freshly-lit fire and went off to the other end of the long oblong room to start making breakfast. She could follow what he was doing just by the sounds. Paper rustling and then a clunk as sliced bread was slid into a toaster.

A fainter click as the kettle went on. Crackling of eggshells and the chatty monologue of an egg frying. He always fried eggs too quickly, so they developed a lacework of bubbles and a black edge.

'Oh, d'you know what . . . ' he said, coming over to the stereo and rifling through discs.

'What would you like?'

'Diminished fifth,' she said. Quite clearly. He looked at her in intense silence, a record in one hand, a teatowel flung over his shoulder.

'Minor Detail?' he suggested. She nodded, wondering again at the scrambled brain cells that could so transpose a band's name. He put on the disc and returned to the cooking, swearing to himself as the fat spat at him.

He had developed a way of feeding the two of them, mouthful about, which ensured that both got hot food, but which required concentration on both parts, and so he now got momentarily touchy when she turned her head away from a proffered bite of toast.

She was looking beyond him at the window of the converted eighteenth-century millhouse.

'Butterflies,' she said. The word was muffled but unmistakable. Her husband sat back in his chair and went through his usual routine.

'Butter? No. Marmalade? Birds? Decorations? Music?'

'Butterflies,' she said again, more firmly.

'Jesus, I can't figure . . . ' he said, baffled.

She butted her head in the direction she wanted him to look, but he was back with the problem of food.

'I'll work it out in a minute, OK?' he said, and inserted toast in her mouth as if he was a postman delivering a letter. For a moment, she considered shoving it back out with her tongue, but sucked it instead. Next time he arrived with a forkful of black lacy egg, she turned her head as far away as she could.

'OK,' he said, ostentatiously patient. 'OK. Butterflies.'

He stood up, turned to the window, and a coloured cloud of them surrounded him. Some of them settled on him, the elaborate primary colours bright against the grey of his cardigan. He stood in startled stillness.

'Butterflies,' he said again, his accent adding a soft aitch after the T so they became buttherflies. There were at least ten of them. He nudged the one on his shoulder so it shifted to the back of his hand, then brought it to her, placing it on the frame that held her wrist rigid. For a few seconds, the russet and ultramarine wings fluttered anxiously, and then were at peace. She watched it for a long time in silence, rehearsing the words so they would come out right.

'At Christmas?'

The man nodded.

'Never heard of that before. Maybe because it's thatched. Maybe the eggs got laid and the warmth of the fire . . . '

He poked the one on his arm until it flew off and settled on the Christmas tree, and then put a fire guard in front of the flames. The room was warmer, now, and the butterflies were flying high in the rafters as if in the branches of a tree in midsummer. She wanted to look more closely at the one on her wrist, but could bring it no closer.

'Tantalus,' she said aloud.

'Yeah,' her husband said, picking up the plates and heading for the sink.

Not being able to get a proper view of the butterfly tainted the pleasure of it being there at all, she realised. It was like having eye-floaters, those oddly shaped images that stay constantly out of visual range, rising and falling with the pattern of one's gaze. Tantalus and the grapes. Or was it grapes? Water, perhaps? And what had been the offence for which the perverse incarceration was the punishment? Her ideas floated ahead of her like a conveyor-belt clothesline decorated with pegs, but moving too fast for garments to be appended thereto. A moment of tumescent misery surged inside her head, pressuring against the hard shell of her skull as the traumatised brain had.

'Tantalus,' she said, more exigently.

'I know bugger all about Tantalus,' he said comfortably, clattering clean plates. 'Nothin'. Empty. White sheet.'

Catching the demand in her face, he closed his eyes to dredge for memories.

'I presume Tantalus is the guy who gave rise to the word tantalise,' he speculated. 'Same as yer man that couldn't push the stone up the hill. Sisyphus. Tantalus had some equivalently frustrating exercise that he couldn't quite fulfill. I'll look it up in the library when we go out.'

She sat silently, the front of her legs beginning to be too warm in the fire heat. He would not remember to look it up, she knew, and she would not remember to remind him. And if she later reproached him, he would laugh and tell her he had more important things to be doing.

'Now, tell me where these go,' he said, kicking off the wheelchair brake and pushing her towards the Christmas tree. Her legs cooled down and she nodded her instructions on where the tinsel baubles should go. The pain was riveting the bones of her face.

'Don't grind your teeth. Makes you look like Desperate Dan in the *Dandy*,' he said.

She watched him open two capsules and empty them into a flat soupspoon filled with yoghurt. He fed the sour mixture to her and a great shudder at the taste ran through her, knocking her plastered legs together and forcing one rigid forearm off the arm of the wheelchair. He lifted the arm back into position without comment. Nor did he make predictions about the painkiller, as her mother would have done.

'You'll feel the good of that in just a few minutes,' her mother would always say. 'You'll never notice the time passing.'

Having dosed her as neatly as a farmer dosing a sheep, he went off to get logs, stepping into wellington boots at the door before heading out into the rainy backyard. For a moment she was filled with fear that the butterflies would follow him out the open door and wilt in the cold outside air, but they stayed where they were. He came back to build up the fire with the sure-handed enjoyment he took in any physical task, sitting back on his hunkers, his hands palmed towards the blaze.

Then the boots were shoved off and he heel-padded in socked feet to wash his hands. One of the butterflies settled on the hot tap, and he tipped it with the back of his hand to get it away.

'Needn't have bothered our arses buying decorations,' he

said, half to himself. 'Free butterflies . . .'

The pain was beginning to ease, keeping in time with her pulse as it retreated.

'Here,' he said. 'Hold these.'

The lightness of the box put into her lap mimicked paper. She pushed with the caged hand at the lid until it came up and off and fell to the floor. The sound of it was swamped in a sudden loud rigour of Gregorian chant from the record player, and her husband's voice jo ined those of the choir.

'*Lumen ad revelationem gentium . . .*'

Six bright silver balls sat, segregated, egg-fashion, in the box, reflecting back six fattened faces at her. Bloated by the convex mirroring, the face was nonetheless different, nose tilted at an angle, forehead dented, the dent rimmed by pale raised scarring. A squealing whimper came through the clenched teeth and the six reflections blurred. Her husband, unhearing, came back to the wheelchair, still singing, and began – deftly – to loop skinny wire hooks onto the baubles.

'Jesus,' he said, breaking off from the male voices. 'Don't *dribble* on the bloody things. Oh. You're crying. Why're you crying?'

The caged hand thumped in demonstration against her chin, then onto the baubles. The voices continued to sing '*Nunc dimittis servum tuum, domine*'.

'Your face, is it?'

She nodded. He mopped her with the teatowel from off his shoulder.

'Yeah,' he said thoughtfully, taking some of the hooked baubles and beginning to position them on the tree. 'I'd forgotten you wouldn't have seen yourself since the accident.'

His tone was casually observant, as if commenting on a one-degree change in external temperature or the lateness of a newspaper. She roared at him in wordless agony, bubbles forming and bursting in the gap between top and bottom teeth. He finished hanging the baubles, came back and mopped her again.

'You have a thing called keloid scarring,' he said informatively. 'That's why the bump on your head has a kind of a rim on it. If you really want to, later, you can have it sort of filed down. But probably if you just grew your fringe a bit longer . . . Other than that, your face is going to be a bit different. But you'll get used to it. I have.'

He took the now empty box off her lap and replaced it with another one. When the lid came off, it was filled with red balls, crusted with metallic grains and non-reflective. After a moment, he resumed the Gregorian chant. When the track ended, for a couple of seconds he hummed the notes again.

'Good singer always hits the notes from above,' he said, quoting some college music teacher he had liked. 'Never *reaches* for them . . . '

You are without sympathy, she thought. You are without imagination. You lack the capacity to truly understand the horror of being behind a strange, distorted face, of knowing that it will never present to the outside world what you are used to it presenting. You have no patience for 'talking out' of problems and your favourite phrase is: 'There's the status quo, and there's worse – which do you want?' You have already got used to my battered face and you will never understand why I should have a problem doing the same. It wouldn't even occur to you to say that you see my face more than I do: you simply don't empathise enough to argue it through at all.

'D'you know what I was thinking?' Her husband was standing over her, dangling a red bauble from its hook. One of the butterflies had settled on it. 'We won't be able to have candles at all. And we'll have to be very careful with the toaster and things like that. I must rig a couple of shields to prevent these lads getting into danger.'

She held out her arms to him and he put his head down on her neck, one arm extended to take care of the butterfly. In a desperation of trust and need, she hugged him awkwardly, hiding her hospital-pale face in the always tanned warm skin of his neck.

'Now,' he said, straightening up as if something had been settled and returning to the task. 'Butterflies and Christmas. What more could we want?'

MARIE-CLARE

CELIA SALKELD

Already the shop windows were displayed for Christmas – full of Santas, reindeers, enormous, costly teddy bears, useful presents for 22/6d, all sparking and skilfully adorned.

Every window twinkled and glittered. One or two of the street vendors had set themselves up, and their mechanical toys were being wound up and put through their paces. The whole town had a bright festive appearance. People looked cold though, cold and harassed.

A sudden icy blast made Marie-Clare wince and pull her fur collar up round her ears. She hated that kind of east wind, it gave her earache. Why on earth hadn't she taken a scarf? Now she'd be sure to get a cold. Of course then, she nearly always did have a cold. Or something. The trouble was friends tended to be unsympathetic. A boy friend had shocked her recently by asking, rather rudely, she thought, if she ever did feel well. He had shocked her into the realisation that people considered her neurotic. Well, what if she were? She couldn't help always feeling awful. It wasn't fair.

She had read a book some months ago, the heroine of which had greatly taken her fancy because she prefaced everything she said with the remark: 'Get me a brandy and soda, darling, I feel horrible.'

It appealed to her so much that she started drinking brandy herself, announcing constantly to her friends. 'Darling, do get me a brandy, I feel horrible.' To her delight, even if they baulked at the expense, it amused them. But only for a while.

She had reluctantly come to the conclusion people didn't like her company. Not that friends left her out of anything. On the contrary. She was definitely accepted as one of them – 'one of the set'. But sometimes the word *tolerated* would come into her mind.

She wanted to be liked. She did her best to please everyone but there was a sort of barrier between herself and other people. She didn't know why it should be so. It made her irritable and resentful.

Life had become a strain to Marie-Clare.

Yet she could go anywhere she liked or do anything that suited her. She earned an excellent salary – designing fabrics for a leading firm – which she spent almost entirely on drink, cigarettes, and expensive clothes. The tedium of everyday bills never encroached on her world. Mummy looked after things like that. When she squandered her salary on some special suit or dress, leaving herself with enough money for a taxi home and little else, good old Mum obligingly came up with the necessary few quid to keep her in drink and cigarettes for the rest of the week.

All her life Marie-Clare had been led to believe that things were her right. She had been indulged by her mother; she was Mummy's little girl. Mummy's little girl who had reached the age of thirty without ever growing up.

She *had* aged though. Her reflection in the mirror no longer reassured. It alarmed her. It alarmed her too the way her female friends were suddenly all either heavily pregnant or about to get married. *She* hadn't really wanted to marry anyone at any time. Leave home? Still . . .

For quite a while now she had given up buying clothes. None of them suited or did anything for her. The endless business of trying them on wearied her and she inevitably came out of a shop feeling on edge, dispirited. Somehow shops always seemed hot and overcrowded nowadays; the whole idea of shopping was intolerable.

Nevertheless today she'd made up her mind to come into town to buy herself some clothes. More than once she had caught friends eyeing a worn elbow. A slightly frayed cuff. Even Mummy had tactfully suggested she should buy herself a nice new dress for Christmas. She must make an effort to improve her appearance, that was all.

Perhaps that was why, as she walked along wondering which shop she'd venture into first, she was feeling worse than usual.

She decided on 'La Mode', the most exclusive one – it wouldn't be so crowded. Besides it would be a relief to get in out of this terrible cold.

Inside, the air, though heavy, was pleasantly scented. Though the shop *was* crowded, human odours didn't seem to pervade it. Everything was neatly and conveniently arrayed. To no avail as far as Marie-Clare was concerned. There was nothing worth buying. A load of expensive Christmas rubbish, she thought crossly, shoving a dress back on its hanger. She had left it too late: it was too near Christmas. A saleslady's frigid 'Is there something wrong, Madam? Can I help you?' sent her scurrying from the shop. At the best of times that species frightened her but this one with her smart black suit, impeccable blue hair, and her superior manner of speaking, had been formidable.

So Marie-Clare, in thoroughly bad humour, found herself once again out on the street. Admittedly she had pulled out every dress in the shop. All the same, how dare the old bitch speak to her like that. A great beginning to the afternoon. Just what she needed. To think of all the money she had spent in that same shop. Well, they could shove their plush carpets and their perfumed air. That was an end of that. Where to go next though? She couldn't stand here shivering on the street indefinitely. Better to forget all about the shopping lark. Just get a taxi and go home. She'd have to come in another day to buy the wretched clothes. But that would be impossible – the shops would be getting even more crowded. No. It was now or never.

Masons, across the street might be worth trying. Mostly their clothes were cheap, badly made. Yet sometimes if you persevered you could find a decent suit or dress hidden away among the rest. At any rate you could pull out everything in the store if you so wished. No one would mind; it was the custom. Grubby hands or not. Masons was a good idea.

Marie-Clare lit a cigarette with some difficulty – her hands were numb with the cold – and inhaled deeply. It made her feel better. Then she pulled her coat tightly round her and crossed over to Masons.

The dress department she knew was on the third floor. Such a mass of humanity filled the ground floor, however, it wasn't a question of going where you wanted. You were carried along by the tide. Swept sometimes into a wrong current out of which you struggled and fought till once more you found yourself heading safely in the right direction. It took some time to get to the first escalator.

As she mounted the second one, panic seized her. God, this was madness. She wouldn't be able to go through with it. She'd die. Somehow she must go back. Get out. She looked back over her shoulder a little wildly. Eyes, cold, challenging, met hers. A relentless procession was coming up behind. There was no escape. Anyway, how ridiculous, she thought. How the hell could you go down when the thing was moving up. She might as well die and be finished with it.

A notice said: 'Dresses size 26-38'. Marie-Clare looked in vain; they were all size 40. She tried the next rack and the one after that. By the time she'd got on to the fourth she had relearned the knack of how to shop efficiently in Masons. You pulled, shoved, if necessary trampled people. You didn't waste time saying please, sorry or excuse me. On and on she went without respite until utterly exhausted, and sweating from the unaccustomed exertions, she stood, one black dress in hand, queuing to get into the fitting room.

The fitting room was simply a corner of the shop curtained off into a line of minute cubicles. There were only two mirrors, one at each end of the line, which necessitated leaving your clothes and your cubicle while you intimately forced yourself through hot female bodies in order to get to the nearest one.

It was chaotic. Women wandered round looking for their clothes, unable to find the right cubicle. Others stripped off boldly beside a mirror, causing dissension by their perspicacity. Children howled, oblivious to mothers' threats. Nerves were raw. Tempers at boiling point. The heat, the lack of air, was unbelievable.

Marie-Clare caught a glimpse of her dress in the mirror and, assured that it fitted – indeed looked remarkably well – had just reached her cubicle when suddenly it happened. Walls, people, curtains, all started to close in on her. For a second everything went black. Then it passed. Her heart thumped violently as she fumbled for her clothes, not caring what way she put them on. Her only thought was to get out.

Unsteady, shaking, she made her way to the cash desk where she handed in the dress and paid for it. Waiting for her change she felt like crying. It was a long time since she'd had such a bad attack.

She was confused, helpless. She couldn't face the mob downstairs for a while yet.

'Eh, Miss! Miss, your change. Maisie, give over that lady's parcel,' the girl was saying. Marie-Clare came sharply to her senses. The Ladies of course. Why hadn't she thought of it before? How stupid. There must be a Ladies.

'Could you tell me where the Ladies is, please?' she asked the girl, accepting her change and her parcel.

'Over there to the right, facing you. Next please.'

She remembered she had a few tranquillisers somewhere in her bag. Perhaps she could get a glass of water. They were difficult to swallow otherwise. Anyway she could stick her head under the tap.

The Ladies room was blessedly cool. Empty apart from a small group round a washbasin. She made straight for the lavatories, paying no heed to them as she passed. She was about to insert her penny when the lavatory attendant, a small dumpy woman in a white overall, came rushing up.

'Use the next one, luv, there's someone in there.'

'Oh, sorry, it said vacant.'

Sitting on the seat, she began to go through the contents of her bag. Slowly and methodically at first but with each second more impatient, becoming aware as she feverishly searched of some slight commotion in the next compartment. She heard the door bang, footsteps, voices going away and then there was silence. Ah, *there* were the pills. Oh thank God, everything would be all right now.

As she shut the door behind her the sobbing started. She paused a moment, startled. It was a child crying. Ah well, no wonder, she thought. It was no doubt weary.

In the washroom, though, such pitiful sobs greeted her that she stopped. The lavatory attendant stood, a glass of water in her hand, in the middle of the group round the washbasin.

'Now, now, everything will be all right. We'll get you home,' she was reassuring.

'What's wrong? Is there a child lost?' Marie-Clare asked, going over. The sobbing stopped. Anxious faces looked at her, surprised by the interruption.

'Ah no,' the attendant answered. 'She's not lost. She's sick.'

A little girl with pigtails, propped up on a chair, was slumped over the washbasin, one side of her face resting on the ledge. Her eyes were closed. A smaller child with red-stained face stood by her, watching apprehensively. Beside them sat a young shabbily-dressed woman, staring at nothing. She seemed dazed, distracted.

'If only I could get her home to the doctor she'd be all right.

If only I could get her home,' she wailed repeatedly.

'Ah now, Mam, you were a very foolish woman to bring that child into town today,' said the attendant. At this the woman burst into an uncontrollable fit of weeping.

'Now Mam, you'll have to pull yourself together. You're only frightening the child going on like that.'

The little figure, crouched over the basin, was beginning to sob faintly, while the smaller child cried loudly and nuzzled up against her. Terrified, they huddled together. The woman wept alone.

'Yes, you must stop crying,' Marie-Clare intervened to the mother. Strange, she thought, that a mother should be so incapable. Was she afraid? Afraid because she knew she had done wrong, bringing the child into town.

'Look, don't worry, we'll get you home. Where do you live?' she asked. The woman blew her nose, making an effort to control herself.

'Oh, it's a long way, Miss, Dolphin's Barn. But I'll not be able to get her as far as the bus. And the queues at this hour. I'll not be able to do it.' She was young, silly, pathetic, sitting there.

'Yes, that *is* a long way but never mind, you could get a taxi.' Realising, as she said it, that this woman had more than likely never taken a taxi in her life. She wouldn't have the money. Awkward, embarrassed, she laid down her parcel and rummaged in her bag.

'Here, please take this,' she said pressing a note into the woman's hand.

'No, no, it's very kind of you but . . . No, I wouldn't take it.'

'Why not? I can spare it.'

'No thank you, it's very kind but . . . '

'Well, I tell you what. I'll get a taxi and leave you home. Will that do?'

'Thanks, that's very kind,' the woman said weakly.

'Is there a phone here?'

'Well, yes.' The attendant looked doubtful. 'You might be able to use the one outside. Look I'll come with ye, Miss.'

The child moaned a little.

'Excuse me just a moment, Miss.' And she turned to the child, placing an arm round her. 'Now luv, I'll leave the water here beside you. Don't worry any more. This lady here is going to get you home and you'll be all right.'

For the first time the little girl raised her head to look directly at Marie-Clare. And Marie-Clare knew that as long as she lived she could never forget that small, grey, death-like face, the large, terror-stricken eyes looking up at her begging reassurance, utterly vulnerable.

The child wasn't just sick, she was gravely ill.

Marie-Clare smiled cheerfully. 'Yes, of course you'll be all right. We'll get you home soon, don't worry.' Wondering, as she spoke, if it were really herself speaking. Herself, Marie-Clare? So useless, so frightened by illness. Speaking brightly. Speaking convincingly, because the eyes looked back at her, temporarily reassured. Believing. Then the eyes closed and the child's head slumped down again exhaustedly.

Marie-Clare glanced back at the others as she followed the attendant out through the door. They were all quiet. Quiet, trusting, waiting.

Just outside the Ladies there was a sort of reception desk at which sat a flashy blonde.

'Excuse me, Miss,' the attendant addressed her humbly. 'There's a little girl sick and this kind lady wants to get her a taxi. Would it be all right for her to use the phone here?'

'We're not allowed calls from here,' the girl answered disdainfully. The little attendant looked suitably cowed. Marie-Clare suppressed her irritation. Better play it cool with this one.

'The child is very sick,' she said, her tone implying that of course she knew the girl would do all she could to help. The blonde reacted.

'Well, I'm sorry, but this is the house phone. You could try the teenager department, there's a phone there.'

'Oh, thank you. Where is that exactly?' But the blonde had turned away from them to inspect her fingernails. That was as far as she was prepared to go.

'I know where it is, Miss. It's way over the other side. I'll show you.' The attendant was herself again. Eager. Ready to go.

Together they set off, battling their way through coats, dresses, people. Once or twice Marie-Clare thought she'd lost her but then she'd appear suddenly from nowhere, by her side again like a small obedient dog. Finally the attendant spotted a supervisor. She re-told her story, while the supervisor regarded Marie-Clare with a mixture of suspicion and curiosity.

'I'm very sorry but our phone is out of order. There's a public phone downstairs. Have you tried that?'

Marie-Clare saw it was hopeless; they could go on trailing

round for ever, getting nowhere, unless she used a different tack.

'Look, I know it's not your fault, but this is nonsense. There is a child sick and we've wasted a lot of time already. Surely there must be a phone somewhere on this floor. I'd like to see the Manageress.' She spoke politely but authoritatively, in a voice which she normally wouldn't dare use – a voice which contained considerable arrogance. The supervisor was clearly at a loss to know what to do. At the same moment a woman in a neat blue suit came towards them.

'I am the manageress, Madam. Can I help you? You can go now,' and she dismissed the supervisor. Again the attendant repeated her story. Again the same doubtful, suspicious looks. Only this time Marie-Clare was being carefully sized up.

'Well, normally we don't allow calls here but I'll ring a taxi for you, if you like. Follow me.' They followed her back to the reception desk. The attendant took her leave.

'I'd better go back now, Miss. I'll tell them that you're getting the taxi.'

'Oh do, yes. Goodbye and thank you for all your help.' It was like parting with an old friend.

The manageress was polite, efficient, but there was something cold and shrewd about her that Marie-Clare didn't like. As she stood there while the manageress waited to be put through to a taxi-rank she felt she was still being assessed – saw the swift searching of her left hand.

No, I'm not married you silly cow, she felt like saying. Why did everyone think it strange that you should want to help another human being? The manageress was speaking.

'Hello, can you send a taxi round to Masons? Excuse me just a moment. What's your name please?'

'Miss O'Neill.'

'It's for a Miss O'Neill. How long will it be? Yes, I'll hold on. And could I have your address please? Thank you,' she said, writing it down. The firm wasn't going to be stuck for a taxi and that was sure. She covered the mouthpiece with her hand.

'By the way, we have a nurse on duty here, you know?'

'No, I'm afraid I didn't know that.'

'Well, I'll send her over now before the taxi comes. Hello, yes, that's fine, thank you. The taxi will be here in five minutes. You'll have to go down and wait for it yourself. Make sure you go to the front door. I'll send them down to you.'

'No, don't do that, I might miss them. I'll come up and let them know as soon as it arrives.'

'Yes, yes, all right. Better go down now. That's the way down over there.' She seemed very anxious to get rid of her.

Marie-Clare wasn't aware of heat or people any more. She was intent only on getting to the main entrance.

Darkness had fallen outside. It was a bitter winter's night now. Still the shop windows shone brightly, lighting up the street. If it weren't for the crowds of people it would have been easy enough to spot a taxi. Marie-Clare had to keep her eyes glued to the street. Cars slowed down, pulled up, and then drove off again. Twice she started forward, seeing a taxi, only to find it was already engaged. Five minutes passed. Then ten. It began to snow. People were hurrying on, taking shelter. The street was getting clearer as a taxi pulled up on the other side of the road. Alert, watching, she saw it immediately and crossed over.

'Are you the taxi that Masons sent for?'

'Yea, that's right.'

'Would you mind waiting for five minutes please. There's a child sick and I'll have to bring her down.'

'Yea, yea.'

The ground floor of Masons was clearer too. In no time she was on the escalator. Like a lunatic she pushed her way up, running, not waiting to be carried. She burst into the Ladies. There was no one there. The attendant looked embarrassed.

'Where are they? I've got the taxi outside.'

'They're gone.'

'Yes, the nurse came and told her to take the child to hospital. That she was very ill. I think she's gone there. There's a hospital not far from here.'

'Are they long gone?'

'Oh, just a few minutes.'

'I might still catch them.'

Surely they'd see the taxi and wait. When she reached the main door, however, there was no one to be seen. She went outside and looked up and down the street. No sign of them anywhere. Returning to the shop she saw a floorman standing near the door. He might have seen them coming out.

'Excuse me, did you see a woman at the door here with two children. One little girl was sick, so she'd probably have been carrying her. I've got a taxi waiting outside and I can't find them.'

'No, Miss, I'm afraid I didn't.'

'Have you been here long?'

'Oh, for the last twenty minutes. I'd definitely have seen them if they came out this way. They might have come down by the lift. You could ask the liftman. It's right over there. He'll tell you.'

'Yes,' the liftman said. 'They came down a few minutes ago. There was a woman and two children. She was carrying one little girl in her arms. The nurse came down with them. Brought them to the door.'

'And did they go out by the main door?'

'Oh no, Miss, the side door. I saw them go myself. They went out the side door.'

'I see, Thank you.'

Marie-Clare walked slowly out of the shop. The taxi had gone. Another, cruising round the corner, pulled up beside her.

'Taxi, miss?'

'No, thank you.' She walked on. It was snowing heavily. She didn't seem to notice. So that was it. The side door. The manageress had done her job well. Get them out. Out of the shop as unobtrusively and as quickly as possible, that was all that mattered. It wouldn't do to have a child so ill there. Why, she might die on the premises! Nobody gave a bloody damn. It was life. And that foolish woman carrying her child out into the snow knew all about it.

On the bus Marie-Clare discovered she had forgotten her parcel. Must have dropped it somewhere, she thought vaguely. But she didn't think of it again. As the bus wound its way through the city out into the pleasant suburbs, all she could think of was the child's face.

She felt strangely reluctant to return to her warm, protective home; and when she reached the house and opened the hall door, she stood, hesitating, as if she might run out into the night again.

'Is that you, Marie-Clare? Poor child, you must be frozen. Come in quick, I'll get you some tea.'

She closed the door. It was too late.

CHRISTMAS FAR FROM HOME

PEIG SAYERS

Christmas Eve fell on a Tuesday and everyone was busy preparing for it. Seáinín came in the door carrying a bundle of ivy and holly.

'Give me a hand, Margaret,' he said, ''till I fasten this to the window.'

'I know nothing about it,' I said, 'because I never saw it done.'

'You'll see it now, girl, and when it'll be fixed up it will be simply beautiful.'

Anna and Eibhlín were busy making paper flowers of every colour; according as they had a flower finished Seáinín would tuck it in among the ivy.

'Bring me the candle now,' he told me.

I got a great red candle and candlestick; this he set on the window-still.

'Make the tea, you,' he told me, 'while I'm fixing up the rest of it.'

I hung the kettle over the fire and while I was waiting for it to boil I fixed the table in the middle of the kitchen. Seáinín told me to get a blue candle, to light it and place it on the table. When I had it lighting I laid the table with delf for the tea. Then Nell got up, and bringing with her three kinds of bread, she sliced it on a bread board. There was plenty jam and butter on the table too and when all the lights were lighting and the kitchen was decorated I thought that I was in the Kingdom of Heaven because I had never before seen such a lovely sight. Nell poured out the tea and everyone sat down to the table; they were all pleasant and cheerful, especially Nell. Every single move her family made filled her with joy.

I was watching them very closely as I drank my tea. Thoughts ran into my mind: I was thinking of my poor mother at that time. I knew the kind of a night she had, a near-sighted, lonely, unfortunate woman without light or joy for I was the one comfort she had in this life. I was far away from her now and I couldn't raise her spirits nor offer her a scrap of happiness.

'The way of the world is strange,' I told myself. 'Look at Nell and the comfort she draws from her family and there are other poor mothers who never get the slightest scrap of satisfaction out of life.'

In spite of all the pleasure around me tears came to my eyes. Seáinín noticed me. 'Margaret is lonesome,' he said.

He came over to me from the other side of the table and began to give me soft talk so as to take my mind off my loneliness.

'Seáinín,' I told him, 'I'm not a bit lonely in the way you imagine, but I was thinking of my mother. Go back and drink your tea.' Then I began eating just like he was.

When we had the supper eaten and all the things were set aside Séamas came in with a bottle of wine and a glass in his hand. 'Would ye like punch?' he asked us.

'We would, Daddy,' the children said. 'This is Christmas Eve!'

'I don't care for wine at all, darlin',' Nan said. 'I prefer a little drop of whiskey.'

Back he went and then returned with a jugful of whiskey.

'Here, take your pick of them!' he said.

Nell made a small drop of wine-negus that was suitable for the family and she gave me a fair jorum of it too.

'Won't you have a drop yourself, Missus?' I asked her.

'I won't, child,' she said. 'I never let a spoonful of drink pass my lips nor would I give it to these children but as little but for respect for the Night that's there.'

'Would you be afraid you'd get drunk?' I asked, for curiosity was picking me.

'Not that, child, but it has always been said: "Taste the food and you'll get fond of it." I don't think there was ever a person who was sipping and tipping at drink but got a mind for it in the latter end.'

Séamaisín and Eibhlín were over at the window-still examining the small lovely pictures that Seáinín had placed here and there. Eibhlín took one of them in her hand and went over where Nan was.

'Nan,' she said, 'look at the nice little Lamb with His feet tied.'

'Aye,' said Nan, 'that's the Blessed Infant whom we all adore tonight.'

'Why does He take the shape of a lamb?' the child wanted to know.

'Sit down there quietly,' Nan said, 'and I'll tell you.' They all sat down.

'At that time a king of high rank called Herod ruled the district where Mary and the Infant were living. He heard about the child Jesus and made up his mind to put to death every male child under the age of three months. He ordered his bodyguard and his soldiers to guard the great city of Bethlehem and not to allow anyone in or out without first finding out all about their business. Immediately the order was received, sentries and guards were posted in very street, at every street corner and on every road and highway. Mary had a close friend called Bríghde and when *she* heard the news she went to Mary who, when she saw her coming, gave her a warm welcome. "Mary," Bríghde told her, "this is no time for talking; it's time to do a good deed." "What's the news now, Bríghde?' Mary asked. "You surely must have heard the dreadful command that Herod has issued? I've come to see if I can think of any plan that will help you to save Little Jesus from the strait He's in." "God will help us, Bríghde," Mary answered. "Get ready so," said Bríghde, "and make no delay. Before daylight in the morning I will dress myself in an *óinseach's* rags and head for such and such a street. Maybe those on guard will follow me; if they do, face southward for the road that leads from the city and perhaps you'll succeed in crossing the bridge of the Great River before anyone challenges you. Goodbye now; I'll be off about my business."

'When Joseph came in Mary told him the whole story from start to finish. The following morning, as it was brightening for day a terrible uproar could be heard outside. A foolish woman was decked out in straw and around her waist was a belt studded with lights and on her head was a ring with twelve candles lighting upon it. She made her way to the point most convenient for Mary to escape. She had a kind of a flute that made an odd sound: as she played the flute the guards were startled and when they raised their heads they saw the witless woman all lighted up. They went towards her, but she kept moving away before them like a gust of wind.

'As soon as Mary got the guards out of the way she set about making her way out of the city. Things went well for her until she came to the bridge across the Great River and there were two soldiers of the guard: they stood right before her on the crown of the road.

'"Where are you off to so early, decent woman?" one of them asked.

'"I've been a week in the city," Mary answered, "and my home is a good distance away. That's why I'm on the road so early."

'"What's that load you have on your back?" a soldier asked again.

'"A little lamb I got to rear as a pet."

'"Maybe this is an excuse," said the other soldier, seizing her and dragging her mantle off her. All he saw was a lamb, its four legs tied with a light cord.

'"See now; she's right," said the other soldier. "It's a great shame for us to delay her."

'Mary was walking on and on until she was free from danger; she sat down in a little corner under a green clump of bushes and lifted Jesus off her back. When she was rested she replaced Him on her back and some time later reached her destination. She now had the Infant safe; a few days afterwards there was appalling desolation and terror because of the slaughter of the little children of the city. The only sound to be heard was the sorrowful crying of the mothers whose children were being put to death by Herod the destroyer. When the dreadful scourge was over Bríghde went out to where Mary was and the pair of women were overjoyed at meeting each other again. They went on their knees and earnestly thanked God for having saved them. Mary could bestow no greater honour on Bríghde than to present her with a feastday. She did so in these words:

"'Your day will come before my day, Bríghde, until the end of the world.'"

'It has been thus ever since and Bríghde's Day comes before Mary's Day and, since there were candles in the plan that Bríghde thought of, candles are blessed in every church throughout the world; "Candlemas Day" it's called.'

'How I love the tiny Lamb!' Eibhlín said.

That love remained in the girl's heart ever afterwards for she offered herself up to the Merciful Lamb and became a nun.

I myself told Nell that Séamaisín, Eibhlín and myself would go to the chapel to see the crib. 'Don't stay there long!' she said.

I caught the children by the hands and off we went. The night was dark but indeed you could pick out the tiniest object on the pavement by the light of all the candles in the windows. When we entered the chapel, praise be to God! it was a beautiful sight with lamps lighting and the altar decorated with a mass of candles all ablaze. The crib was at the side of the altar and if you were the dullest person who ever lived it would remind you of the Kingdom of Heaven. The nuns were playing sweet hymns and my heart was filled with joy and pleasure as I listened to music the likes of which I had never heard before.

I scrutinised everything around me so that I didn't find the time passing. I got a start when I heard the thump of Séamaisín's head hitting the altar rail; the poor little man was falling asleep.

'Let's go home, darling,' I said, 'you're sleepy.'

It was ten o'clock when we arrived home.

'Sit down here now,' Nell said, 'I have boiled milk and sweet cake for ye.'

She didn't put me in a place where I'd feel humbled and I had my share as well as the rest. Before we were ready Seáinín and his father came in after having been out for a stroll.

'*Sha*, let's go on our knees in the name of God and say the rosary,' Nan said.

When we were finished: 'Off to sleep with ye now, my little clan,' Séamas said.

There was no need for him to say it a second time. They went upstairs to bed. I remained on with Nell and Séamas in the kitchen until twelve o'clock and we had a great deal of chat and pleasant company.

From *Peig*

Translated from the Irish by Bryan MacMahon

ON THE SECOND DAY OF CHRISTMAS

MÁIRE WALSH

Nancy felt proud as she sat in the driver's seat. Having passed her test, she wouldn't be under a compliment to anyone this year. Polly, holding the eleven months' old baby, felt safe – there was room for both of them beside the driver. Her three other brothers in the back were pushing and shoving, all wanting to be behind their mother. Directly the dinner was over they had left so as to spend plenty of time visiting seven cribs on this St Stephen's day.

Three miles out the road they stopped at the first church, St Anne's, called after the Blessed Virgin's mother. Entering by the stile in the stone wall surrounding the chapel yard was easier than lifting the iron gates. Like a clutch of clucking hens the trio rushed to climb over the gates, not listening to their mother's rebuke. As she handed the baby over the stile to Polly, Johnny fell. The others laughed as she wiped the bleeding knee with her headscarf.

It was bright inside with the daylight coming through the stained-glass windows. Homely and sacred. From her pocket she handed them pennies to light candles. After watching them with a young mother's pride, they knelt before the crib, the children chattering while she and Polly prayed. The baby crawled into the straw, pushing some into his mouth, then spitting it out. Holy innocence. As Polly prayed with her eyes shut she envied angels. They didn't have to carry heavy babies.

'Come on now, boys, hurry. Polly, you let the child crawl into the crib, take him out.'

'Bold, bold, baba,' said Polly. 'We should have left you at home.'

Nancy genuflected with reverence, then beckoned to them to follow her. They had a long journey before them. This custom had been handed down on her father's side of her own family. On his dying bed he asked her to promise him that she would continue visiting the seven cribs. She didn't deny him his wish; she supposed whether or which, she would have done so of her own accord. It gave her a spiritual uplift which always stood her well from one Christmas to another.

St Dympna's stood at the crossroads next to the school-house. A small church for a scattered population. The crib was situated under the stairs in a cramped area. Dull, with little imagination, where you couldn't linger for long with the draught behind you. Polly felt sad. She wished there was a place for it near the altar. They lit a few more candles, and when the mother was doing the stations, they lit more without any pennies. She was vexed, telling them it was as good as stealing. She made them blow them out. Teach them honesty when young as she was taught herself. All three blew them out, all out, as if it were a birthday cake. She relit the ones they paid for while Polly stood anxiously facing the door. She felt mortified lest someone would come in.

The next church had no crib so they passed it. The ICA ladies were holding a dance this coming year for funds for an elegant crib which they were to import from Italy. A good thing, it would take a few miles off their journey. Darkness would be falling soon. When they pulled up at the mountain parish church, two ladies were talking outside. Nancy thought they'd never move. She waited until they left, exactly twenty-five minutes by her watch. The three lads in the back were uneasy to get out so as to run around the graves. She couldn't let herself down by letting them run wild. Not in front of *them*. Women with families reared and gone. More to say than they had to eat. Observant faggots that could tell by your drawn face that you were seven weeks on the way, before you had time to ask the doctor. They wouldn't have the satisfaction now, news like this was soon enough for Polly to hear. Out loud they'd talk about praying that it would be a girl.

Once inside, the young trio made for the galleries. First up played the organ. A litter of kittens could have done a better job. Doh, doh, doh, la, la, la . . . jingle bells, jingle bells . . . now a fit of giggling. The mother called them. They should be strapped like a dog, then she'd have full control. Every year seemed harder than the last. The candle money went into the crib donation box to put towards a new shepherd. It was they who had broken it by accident when they tried to ride the donkey. Fr Murphy said, 'What harm, they'll only be young once.' The crib with only one shepherd had a paling around it this year. Fr Murphy wasn't taking any more chances.

'Come down out of that, you villains,' called Nancy.

They gave her the deaf ear. Polly ran up, belting them down again. St Joseph grimaced at the noise of their clattering footsteps. The Blessed Virgin looked up to heaven, or so Nancy thought as she tried to pray. The baby crept on all fours, scraping the skin off his knees. Polly picked him up without a moan.

Patient with him while he tried to wriggle down again. Only for her, Nancy wouldn't have managed at all.

The fourth church lay in a valley down a long winding lane. Overgrown hedges were almost bare of leaves, a lone magpie darted from a branch in front of them. A bad omen. Maybe they would meet another. None came. A cloud of fear descended on Nancy. She could hear her father's voice somewhere, telling her to take heart. Polly sensed her fears and told her not to fret.

'Everything comes to those who wait and pray.'

'Who told you that?'

'Sr Martha.'

Well then, Sr Martha had a candle lit for her unbeknownst to her. A pity they didn't think of asking her to come, she'd have helped with the baby. Nancy's thoughts were working overtime. She felt frustrated, sorry they came at all. The trio were now less lively, but moving about nevertheless. Nancy did the stations at a slower pace. If only the children could remain still like the figures of the crib. They'd have to be dead.

They continued their itinerary southwards, facing for home. The Franciscan friary in a fairly large village was their favourite church. People were going in and out all the time paying visits. Warm and cosy, with three sets of candle holders. The one nearest the altar had three rings of candles. This they considered a rich crib. The lifesize figures were awe-inspiring. Well back into a niche in the wall, no one could touch them. The Angelus bells rang six as they were leaving. At this rate of going it would be near eight when they'd get home. Where did the time go? Nancy hurried to The Chapel of Ease where a dotey little crib stood, made of ice-pop sticks. More like a doll's house. Toy-like figures all crowded into a small space. Dark and dreary except for the glow of a bicycle lamp stuck in the straw. After saying only one Hail Mary they left.

St John's and St James's was about an hour's journey from there. A pair of hikers stopped her for a lift which she gladly gave them, more for the company than anything else. It was raining hard. They were grateful. The man remained silent as his girlfriend told how they had lost their way, taken the wrong road, which they didn't realise until they were too far from the main road to go back. The guest-house lady would be expecting them already, they could find their own way after reaching the church. Nancy wouldn't hear tell of them walking the rest of the way, putting herself out a few more miles. They'd never been inside a Catholic Church, much less visit a crib. Polly offered thanks to God for saving their souls.

By the time they were visiting this last church they were tired and hungry. Then misfortune in the way of a puncture took them unawares. Out they got to thumb a lift, with the rain pelting down. The first few cars were full already and sped on. They could see by the dim lamp of their own car. After eleven cars passed Nancy decided to put the family back into it, she'd have a better chance by herself. The driver in the next car must have thought she was a whore, the way he hurried past. Maybe with the baby in her arms she'd have better luck. He cried and bawled with hunger. She decided then that maybe they should walk home. At some stage they were bound to get a lift. Johnny got piggybacked by the twins in turn until they could stick it no longer. Darkness, lonesomeness, and fear sickened them.

'Mammy, I want to do wee wee,' wailed Johnny. They all wanted to. She put her hand into her pocket for the matches to make a light. They were in St Dympna's. Mother of God, what was coming over her memory? The doctor told her to take things easy, didn't he. Polly managed the buttons for them as best she could. What difference if she left them alone, they were soaking wet already with rain. Nancy thought of a plan. She told Polly to come a bit down the road, leaving one twin holding the baby, the other Johnny. When the next car would come in sight, both of them would stand in the middle of the road with outstretched arms to stop it.

It came from the opposite direction. The driver screeched to a halt. A bedraggled pair of tinkers, he didn't like the look of the bloodstained scarf on the woman's head. If he took them in they'd give trouble, he felt sure.

He opened the window and said, 'Yes?'

'Excuse me, sir, we can't get a lift home. Could you oblige us, it isn't far into the town. We're worn out walking, sir.'

'Sorry,' he said, looking straight out in front of him. 'Can't you see I'm making for Athlone. Someone going your way will see you right.'

Polly opened the back door and got in. Nancy defiantly remained at the front as she called the little ones. They didn't budge. They were frantically calling for her. Tears were streaming down her own face. Polly prayed out loud to the Infant Jesus. The man could hardly believe his ears. Then she stopped with a sigh before asking him if he would change the wheel.

He softened. They had a car, then they must be respectable.

His nylon shirt stuck to his back with the perspiration that overcame him. The spirit of his dead mother's soul haunted him. Christmas was a hateful time for him, always was. His conscience seemed to be on fire. How did the blood come on her scarf? Frail sickly woman. Miserable wound-up child saturated with religion, soiling the upholstery with her wet clothes. He was trapped.

'No one wants to know the poor. You think we are poor, we have land, acres of it – you with your car not paid for – I know your kind – you don't have to tell me. I'd walk every inch of the way only for the weight of the baby, *is trom cearc abhfadh, is trom cearc abhfadh* . . . do you understand, sir?'

Words mightier than his pride, hurt pride now. Nancy remained where she stood as he drove the car to where the children lay in a heap alongside the ditch, like figures in a crib. Polly guided them one by one into the comfort of the car. He drove slowly as he turned to collect the mother. Not a word was spoken between them until he left them safely home.

'Would you like to come in for a sup of tea?' asked Nancy. He shook his head, as if he was shaking the dust off them.

'Then thanks very much for your trouble, and may the Infant Jesus and His Holy Mother guide you on your journey.'

She could swear to God that she heard him say 'Christ'.

WHITE CHRISTMAS, 1953

MOY McCRORY

It was the time when she first gave birth that had hardened her against any sentiment. God, how she had suffered to bring their son into the world. And she had been terrified, left on her own in that miserable room; it didn't seem right, not on her first ever time. She had even begged that nasty nurse to stay out of desperation. That bitch!

'You are not the only woman to be having a baby,' she told her. 'I've got other younger women making less fuss than you!' and she flounced out, leaving Nell frightened and miserable, scolded like a schoolchild with tears beginning to well up in shame for her self-pitying nature. Then the pain would start again.

'Jesus, Mary and Joseph!' she screamed. 'Help me! Help me!'

But no one did. When a nurse finally came, it was to tell her off. She put her head round the door.

'Oh, stop shouting, you silly girl!' she said and withdrew.

Nell was crushed. Forty-one was too old to be having a first baby. Everyone had told her that and filled her with anxiety.

'Anything could go wrong,' her unmarried sister said, but no one told her what. She had gone in the first time expecting to die. She thought that was why they were leaving her alone.

He came in the day after, tired from work. Her eyes stared

emptily at him. She had touched depths of fear previously unknown and had been shocked. She felt resentful. What did he
know? Him and his bloody work. She felt then as if she hated
him. She blamed him. It hadn't been what she expected. They
would not let her see the boy for two days. They said it would
upset her. He was covered in bruises from where the doctor had
clamped and pulled and pulled. The violence of it was horrifying,
everyone shouting instructions at once, screaming at her as though
she had done something bad. She felt castigated. She had been
punished more than adequately. And soft lad at work, getting off
scot free. Christ! Men had it easy, no doubt about it. If they felt
a tenth of the pain, they would insist on all families stopping at
one.

Nine days before Christmas she had given birth to her
second child, a girl. She did not know it then, but this daughter
was also to be her last. She was only aware of the cramps in her
womb each time she put the baby to her breast and watched
it suck urgently, as if it already sensed that this blissful state
would be soon curtailed.

Jet black the little one's hair had been, long enough to
cover the head as she emerged, wet and glossy, and puffed up
with her mother's hormones.

Nell's sister, on her only visit to the hospital, had started
laughing as soon as she saw the child. 'It's got a bust. Look!'
she exclaimed, surveying the child's chest through the deep
square neck of the regulation gown that had slipped off its
shoulders. She was amused to see a tiny new-born one with
such apparent maturity, rushing towards adulthood.

In two days, the hair had already begun to lighten and drop

out and the swelling was subsiding. The red mottled face grew paler. The baby was changing overnight and Nell didn't always feel sure when she went into the nursery that she would select the right one; she couldn't stop herself from checking the name tag each time.

He had come in to visit on the same evening after the child had been born and saw for the first time his tiny daughter.

'She's beautiful,' was all he managed to say as he saw the delicate feet kicking the air and watched her mouth trying to taste the world around it. He was speechless with genuine delight. Nell looked at his face.

Soft bugger, she thought. It was all a mystery to him – he could afford to be in awe – she was the one with the stitches. She did not have feelings left to marvel with, they had been pummelled out of her.

She watched his back now as he walked out of the ward. She knew that she would not see him again for a while. He was working nights and it was difficult to get to the hospital, and the strict visiting hours did not help.

The baby grunted. She lifted it over to the other side. Fifteen minutes each way. She kept a close watch on the clock. She did not like feeding, but it was only for the first few weeks so she could endure it. They told her the first time that she did not have enough milk and they must have seen plenty of mothers to know; besides, a bottle was more hygienic.

During the day she would lie on the bed staring around the ward. Everything was white: all the hospital linen, the bed covers, the shifts they brought her for the baby, even the little blanket she wrapped the child in. Only the walls were different.

Painted just a fraction off white, they were a pale cream, but sometimes even they looked the same. Nell would stare as everything merged together without boundary or edge, limitless without borders: the walls, ceilings, sheets, beds, even the baby and herself. She thought she might be going mad. Even the sky, when she glimpsed it through the windows, was colourless as if all blood had been drained from the day.

She continued to bleed heavily. She wondered when it would stop. But it was all that broke the monotony, the occasional cluster of red stains on the sheets when the nurses came to change the bed.

She had been there nearly five days when they came to tell her she was being moved.

'Get your things,' the staff nurse told her.

'Am I going into another ward?'

All around her women were packing small toilet bags, equally unprepared. They had been told to send their suitcases home the first night.

'There isn't room to keep that,' the ward sister had told Nell when she arrived at the labour ward on the arm of the ambulance driver. 'Where is your husband? Out in the corridor? You will have to give it to him to take home.'

Nell was writhing as the stronger surges of pain gripped her. The ward sister was angry because Nell did not have a husband conveniently waiting in the corridor who could take care of everything.

'He's working nights, it's the shift,' she tried to explain, but the woman had towered over Nell, making her feel stupid and terribly wrong. She was scared to argue or say anything. The one time she had asked for help she had been shouted at; it made her wonder if any demands in hospital were unreasonable. She did not want to be a troublemaker, and hadn't the midwife scolded her for making too much fuss?

'You're being moved to Southport,' the nurse at the desk informed her. 'Sign here. It's just a formality. Have you got everything?'

Nell carried a brown paper bag in one hand, containing a tube of toothpaste, a comb and some hair curlers. Her hair was an irritation, fine, sparse and grey. She put rinses in to keep it brown, but the roots must have come though by now because she had not done it for weeks, but it was the least of her worries.

'Why am I being moved?'

The nurse looked up from writing, surprised to see that Nell was still there. 'You're not the only one,' she said, continuing to write.

'I can see that, but why are we being moved?'

'Overcrowding. We're expecting ten new admissions this weekend. We need the beds. You're being sent to a nursing home.'

Later that morning Nell was bundled up and the baby brought out of the nursery and given her to hold. It was the longest time she had nursed her child as she was pushed along lying on a trolley, staring up at the ceiling, feeling disorientated. How would he know where she was? Nobody in her street had a telephone, not even the corner shop, and when they asked her if she knew his work number she thought they meant his national insurance at first. She could not even remember the name of the factory he had been sent to that week.

'Never mind, we'll tell him on his next visit,' they said brightly, as she was called. But when would that be? Two, three days? She felt unnerved. Her sister had come over from Ireland, but she was busy looking after Nell's son while her husband worked. She could hardly get in in the evenings. They would not allow children in the wards and the boy was too small to be left on his own outside. But if it was not awkward enough already, how would Joe ever get to see her in Southport?

He'd have to get the train from Exchange Station, and a bus, two buses, one either side. It would take him hours and he would not be able to stay, on account of getting all that way back again. It would be impossible for him to come, and unreasonable for her to expect it. She felt lonely already. It would be days before anyone knew where she was. He would only find out on his next visit and between then she would be out in Southport without a living soul knowing her whereabouts. It was a frightening thought.

Suppose something happened to him at work, suppose the police came to the hospital? She did not trust the nurses to remember who she was, or to give the correct information. Maybe she could write to him, save him the shock of turning up and seeing another woman in the bed. But she would need pen and paper and a stamp. Could she get them in the nursing home? Her mind raced with anxiety. She could always give the letter to a visitor to post; not the staff, if they were anything like this place they would just forget. She would look for someone sympathetic and go up and explain that she had just been moved.

She relaxed her grip on the baby and breathed a little easier now that at least she had a plan.

At the end of the corridor Nell was lifted up and put on a stretcher, a heavy blanket placed over her, and she was carried outside. She felt powerless.

'Hang on a minute, love,' one of the bearers said as they gently laid the stretcher down on the firm snow beside the ambulance. They said something to her, but she did not catch it. All she heard was the soft thud as the stretcher touched snow, and she knew that she was alone. The men had left her to look for something, keys or a watch. She lay cuddling her baby under the blanket, staring at the winter's sky and people's feet as they passed her in the hospital grounds. It was a strange view of the world. She felt very small, dwarfed by life around her until she looked down and saw her tiny child.

The temperature had dropped, cold enough for snow, it felt like it would freeze. Overnight the roofs would ice up and pipes burst in homes all over Liverpool. She held the baby close to her to retain body heat, beginning to feel scared in case she had been abandoned, left on her back with a five-day-old baby. She could see the headlines already. 'Irish woman found frozen to death outside Liverpool Hospital. New baby in intensive care machine. Horrified father says he was working nights.'

She wrapped her arms tighter about the tiny thing so that it might not feel the cold. Nell was worried that the baby would become ill and she squeezed it to herself in panic.

'If anything happens to this child, troublemaker or not, I'll go back in there and strangle the nurse with my own bare hands, the one that made me sign the form. See if I don't!'

When she looked around for signs of the men returning, all she could see was the cold, clean, clinical snow. White. She was entombed in it. Only the path showed through, a living trail of black asphalt. Snow begin to fall again, she was aware of it tickling her face, then dampening her hair. She watched the baby licking snowflakes with its new pink tongue and for one giddy moment felt herself sinking as if she had just come to the end of a fall, when the weight of her body would jar in her knees, as she struggled to stay upright. But she was not upright, she was lying down, or had been. The ground under her was spinning. Thank God for the snow on it, at least it would be soft to fall in. But she did not fall. She pushed the baby down under the blanket so that its face was protected and clasped the little white bonnet tightly to its head. The few wisps of dark hair escaping from it were like slashes, deep, dark and shocking. She focused all her attention on her child's black hair. The white sky was moving again. She felt her sense of balance being upset, so she concentrated on her daughter's safety. It took her a long time to realise that the men had returned and it was they who must have lifted her. She was back inside the ambulance and could not remember getting there. She heard the engine warming up and the slow movement of the wheels as they turned down the drive. All the way to Southport she lay on her back where they had placed her. She could not see out. The baby slept and, lulled by the sound of the engine, Nell dozed.

She was lonelier than she had ever been in Southport. No one came to visit her. They recommended after the birth that she stay in for two weeks, which was normal practice and she knew that he would not be able to come on Christmas Day because there was no transport. If she had been in Liverpool he would have walked into the hospital or taken a taxi, but all the way to Southport, that was a different matter. Maybe her sister would come on Christmas Eve, but that would mean leaving Brendan with a neighbour and it would be awkward.

She missed her little son all the more for knowing that she would not be able to see him. She felt sorry for her husband too, rushed off his feet all the time, having to leave his son with someone so he could get out to work. It was good of Bridget to offer to stay with them and help them through this time, but Nell was worried because her husband never liked Bridget, and she could imagine the atmosphere at home.

Bridget held him responsible. He made Nell go through all this a second time when the first birth had almost killed her. Bridget said that men were pigs. Older than Nell, she was unmarried. She had no time for men and physical contact with them, sex, was horrific to her. To Nell it was not much better, but it was no longer a mystery. She had the knowledge which struck terror into Bridget's wild imagination. The sisters would have been ashamed to speak to each other about such matters and Nell felt sullied in her sister's gaze.

They had gone down to meet her at the Pier Head, Nell large and cumbersome, slowly following Joe. He had been the one to spot Bridget out of the crowds pouring down the gangplank.

'Stand back against the wall,' he shouted to his wife. 'Stay by the gates, we'll come out to you.'

There was such a crush she could easily get hurt. She stood back and then she saw them coming up over the cobbled stones where the buses picked up passengers for Lime Street. Joe was carrying Bridget's suitcase and Nell could see that neither spoke to the other as they walked stiffly along, without pleasantries to take the edge off their meeting.

Nell had not wanted to wait outside, for it allowed her sister to scrutinise her from such a length. She wanted to be on top of her so that Bridget would not have time to stare at her disgusting belly. She felt coarse, red-faced and common. Bridget was slim. Always had been. Her hair was still dark and thick, and she had put it up in a roll on the back of her head. She looked strict and efficient, like a schoolteacher.

She knew that Joe would be having a harder time under Bridget's cold stare. This time Bridget had an air of contempt about her, letting Nell know that she only had herself to blame. Bridget disapproved of their marriage right from the start and, being the eldest, had a right to say so. She was fond of airing her opinions. She could do so without words, just a look, a gesture of hopelessness towards Joe, and he would understand and be awkward and wary in his own home. It was not right. Nell's eyes felt hot. She so wanted them to be together this Christmas; it was her family, she was a mother with two children now and a husband. Her sister did not fit into any of her calculations, she was the visitor who came among them and made them nervous.

She had not wanted it to be like this. She thought Christmas would be lovely this year with a new baby, but the practical matters had stopped any celebrating, keeping her prisoner and trapping him. It was not right. In her arms she held what was to be the most precious Christmas present ever. She wanted to give him his daughter on Christmas Day; her gift. It had, after all, been worth it and this little one had been so eager to be born, not like the boy who hung back timidly, reluctant to explore. He wanted the certainty of her womb; unlike this one who had hardly given her time to count between contractions, the pain coming so fast, and suddenly she was there yelling, still in a hurry.

Joe could not get out to Southport so he had sent her a pound note to buy things she might need. She spent it on women's magazines and bars of chocolate from the counter in the foyer. She never spent money on herself like this, she was thrifty through necessity and would not dream of wasting it, but she felt desperate for comfort and each time she parted with a coin, a little shiver of excitement ran up her back. She had spent a whole half-crown one day and could not stop herself from grinning as she scurried back to the small ward with the other nursing mothers. There were times when it felt as though it was part of a strange holiday that she had not chosen for herself.

He sent her a Christmas card. When she opened it a five-pound note fluttered out. She stared at it in amazement. He must have been feeling rotten. She had an idea.

'Get yourself something,' he had written inside. She decided to get a taxi.

She was supposed to stay in for six more days, it was usual, but she felt fine and the baby was healthy. She reasoned that if she had given birth at home no one would have made her go away for two weeks. The two weeks was supposed to build her up; solid food placed in front of her, more meat than she had ever seen, and a warm dry nursery for the baby. When she thought about the damp at home her resolve wavered; was she being selfish wanting to rush the baby out of comfort and let it discover early that she had not been born with anything remotely resembling a silver spoon?

It was Christmas Eve. Nell stood in the entrance hall with a brown paper carrier bag.

'I don't care,' she told the charge nurse that morning, 'I'm going home and that's that. He can't get up here for Christmas and by the time I write to him asking for my clothes the holiday will be over. I'll go the way I am. Please, I want to be home for Christmas.'

She stood in the hall wearing her overcoat over her night-dress. She did not have a dressing-gown and for the first time she was glad of the fact.

'I understand,' the nurse said to her. 'Just sign here will you, it's an acknowledgement of your responsibility. Nothing important, just a formality,' and she smiled. Nell was sure that it was the first time she had seen one of them smile.

As she waited in the entrance a group of junior nurses walked past. One shouted back to her, 'Have a lovely Christmas,' and Nell noticed how their eyes became strangely glassy as they saw her standing with her baby. Christmas was after all a time for families.

Behind Nell the holy family stood in tableau. The ass's head which peeped out from behind a holy man genuflecting, was nothing more than a head cleverly stuck into a block of wood, so that viewed from the front it appeared to be a complete animal. The committee which had donated the crib had managed as best they could with limited resources. Nell thought that it was lovely. The Christ child lay in an orange box with bits of straw strewn around to make it look authentic, although the words 'first grade tomatoes' appeared down the side of the makeshift manger. Supposed to be the image of life, the statue was heavy and lifeless. Its over-plump arms were modelled into wrinkles which were no longer desirable in a child. Paint flaked from them. It looked convincing enough to Nell, it made her shudder, especially when icy blasts from the entrance door blew across its bare torso.

A group of schoolchildren were doing the rounds singing carols in the wards. Their high voices reached out into the corridor.

> Hark the herald angels sing
> Glory to the new-born king.
> Peace on earth and mercy mild
> Christ and sinners reconciled.
> Hark the herald angels sing
> Glory to the new born king.

It rang in her head, playing over and over all the way back in the taxi. She knew that she was being reckless. She tried not to look at the meter as it ticked away. It stood at three and six before they had even left the nursing home grounds. Christmas rates! There was no way of stopping the machine and little

106

point in making herself anxious about it. She stared at the meter, hating it and hoping to put it off, but it coolly registered another sixpence. She ignored it. The Christmas spirit was taking her over.

Glory to the new-born king!

She clutched her own new-born child to her and loved it angrily. She was part of the Christmas message, hers was the model holy family. She felt that she could have run all the way back to Liverpool or flown on the feathery wings of the herald angels.

She put her key in the door. All the way home she had anticipated his reaction. She was going to wish him happy Christmas and give him his daughter to hold. He might even cry. She would turn away, she would not mind. They would both stay up late together after Bridget had gone to sleep and fill their son's stocking for Christmas morning, Bridget would have made sure that there was plenty of small things for that, and the baby would sleep in her own little cot for the first time. It was going to be lovely. She turned the key and pushed the door open. The house was silent. Bridget must have taken the boy out. She was late bringing him back, but Nell was not worried, Bridget would have him warmly wrapped up against the weather. She stepped inside.

Something felt different. She smelt paint. She sniffed. Fresh paint, he must have been redecorating as a surprise. No wonder he'd been tired when he came to the maternity hospital the first time. He must be getting one of the rooms ready, she thought delightedly. At last they would have another bedroom and they would move their son into it and let the baby sleep at the foot of their bed. They would not all have to sleep on the same room. Maybe he had got the damp looked at, maybe he'd paid someone to replace the floorboards after all. But behind the paint there was a fusty smell of old damp that she knew too well. The smell of mould underlying everything. In one breath she took it all in, the rotting wood upstairs, damp, dust and fresh paint. But something was not right, she felt it. There was too much paint for one thing, it was overpowering, and the house was too quiet.

She walked slowly up the dark lobby and flicked on the switch, its click announcing her like an intruder in the still house. Where was everybody? It felt very cold. Under the kitchen door came a chilling draught which caught her ankles, ludicrous in fur slippers. She pulled her coat around her; the thin nightdress underneath made her feel naked. She was scared. If she opened the door and went into the kitchen she would see everything. She stood without moving. There was still time. She could creep back out through the front door and bolt away down the street before she had made any discovery. But what would she do? Go back to the nursing home? They would not take her back; she had signed a form, and anyway, one of the neighbours might see her and wonder what she was up to in her nightdress. With brooding anticipation she knew that she had to stay. She edged the kitchen door open and peered around.

As far as she could see, everything was white. She could not believe it. White paint dripped out of an empty tin hanging upside down from a ladder. The lino was covered with splashes spreading from the centre like a giant white chrysanthemum which unfolded its snowy petals as the paint spread across the floor. A plank was balanced across two ladders, while another had come unhitched and lay half-propped up against the wall. A piece of sandy tarpaulin was drenched in emulsion and lay discarded. White had splattered up the walls; and the settee, which he had not covered, was ruined. The rest of the furniture he had bundled into one corner and thrown a sheet over, but she saw how the chair legs which protruded had been sprayed.

Nell stared; there was so much white, she thought that she was back lying in the snow. She began to reel with horror and caught the wall with one free hand to steady herself. Her palm was coated in the emulsion. She opened her mouth to scream and saw the back door suddenly blow open. Joe stood there in the cold wiping paint off himself with a rag. He bent down and began to heave a bucket of water up the steps. It splashed, soaking his feet. He was cleaning up the catastrophe. As he looked up he saw her and froze. His carefully planned surprise had backfired.

Nell stood there stupidly, her eyes round with dismay. She looked as though she might cry. That would be the final insult to him; that she should turn up unexpectedly and blame him for not being prepared. He crashed his paint brush down on the yard step and swore at her. He had a foul temper when things did not go according to plan. He blamed everyone else for things which went wrong. If only they would leave him to himself, he used to say. Then he could get things done, finish jobs, without all this bloody interference. He could never get to the end of a job in peace. He was sick of it, he had put up with a week of her bloody sister, he was not going to let her start on him after that.

'Why the bloody hell couldn't you have stayed in for another week!' he yelled.

For a second, her eyes met his and he saw and recognised in them that strange, empty look he had seen once before and never been able to forget. The look with which she greeted him on the birth of their first child, when, in the moment before she stared past him as if he was not there, she had fixed on him a glance of total condemnation, before dismissing him from her life for good. Now Nell was staring past him again, her eyes empty. She felt her heart blanch as all feeling in her turned away from him. All feeling, for he had hurt her in a way that she could not understand and once again she was shocked by the force of her suffering. The baby, aware of nothing but its own hunger, began to cry.

OWENEEN THE SPRAT

EDITH Œ. SOMERVILLE AND MARTIN ROSS

I was labouring in the slough of Christmas letters and bills, when my wife came in and asked me if I would take her to the Workhouse.

'My dear,' I replied, ponderously, but, I think, excusably, 'you have, as usual, anticipated my intention, but I think we can hold out until after Christmas.'

Philippa declined to pay the jest the respect to which its age entitled it, and replied inconsequently that I knew perfectly well that she could not drive the outside car with the children and the Christmas tree. I assented that they would make an awkward team, and offered, as a substitute for my services, those of Denis, the stopgap.

Those who live in Ireland best know the staying powers of stopgaps. Denis, uncle of Michael Leary the Whip, had been imported into the kennels during my ministry, to bridge a hiatus in the long dynasty of the kennel-boys, and had remained for eighteen months, a notable instance of the survival of what might primarily have been considered the unfittest. That Denis should so long have endured his nephew's rule was due not so much to the tie of blood, as to the privileged irresponsibility of stopgap. Nothing was expected of him, and he pursued an unmolested course, until the return of Flurry Knox from South Africa changed the general conditions. He then remained submerged until he drifted into the gap formed in my own establishment by Mr Peter Cadogan's elopement.

Philippa's Workhouse Tea took place on Christmas Eve. We were still hurrying through an early luncheon when the nodding crest of the Christmas tree passed the dining-room windows. My youngest son immediately upset his pudding into his lap; and Philippa hustled forth to put on her hat, an operation which, like the making of an omelette, can apparently only be successfully performed at the last moment. With feelings of mingled apprehension and relief I saw the party drive from the door, the Christmas tree seated on one side of the car, Philippa on the other, clutching her offspring, Denis on the box, embosomed, like a wood-pigeon, in the boughs of the spruce fir. I congratulated myself that the Quaker, now white with the snows of many winters, was in the shafts. Had I not been too deeply engaged in so arranging the rug that it should not trail in the mud all the way to Skebawn, I might have noticed that the lamps had been forgotten.

It was, as I have said, Christmas Eve, and as the afternoon wore on I began to reflect upon what the road from Skebawn would be in another hour, full of drunken people, and, what was worse, of carts steered by drunken people. I had assured Philippa (with what I believe she describes as masculine *esprit de corps*) of Denis's adequacy as a driver, but that did not alter the fact that in the last rays of the setting sun I got out my bicycle and set forth for the Workhouse. When I reached the town it was dark, but the Christmas shoppers showed no tendency to curtail their operations on that account, and the streets were filled with an intricate and variously moving tide of people and carts. The paraffin lamps in the shops did their best, behind bunches of holly, oranges, and monstrous Christmas candles, and partially illumined the press of dark-cloaked women and more or less drunken men, who swayed and shoved and held vast conversations on the narrow pavements. The red glare of the chemist's globe transformed the leading female beggar of the town into a being from the Brocken; her usual Christmas family, contributed for the festival by the neighbours, as to a Christmas number, were grouped in fortunate ghastliness in the green light. She extracted from me her recognised tribute, and pursued by her assurance that she would forgive me now till Easter (i.e. that further alms would not be exacted for at least a fortnight), I made my way onward into the outer darkness, beyond the uttermost link in the chain of publichouses.

The road that led to the Workhouse led also to the railway station; a quarter of a mile away the green light of a signal post stood high in the darkness, like an emerald. As I neared the Workhouse I recognised the deliberate footfall of the Quaker, and presently his long pale face entered the circle illuminated by my bicycle lamp. My family were not at all moved by my solicitude for their safety, but, being in want of an audience, were pleased to suggest that I should drive home with them. The road was disgustingly muddy; I tied my bicycle to the back of the car with the rope that is found in wells of all outside cars. It was not till I had put out the bicycle lamp that I noticed that the car lamps had been forgotten, but Denis, true to the convention of his tribe, asseverated that he could see better without lights. I took the place vacated by the Christmas tree, the Quaker pounded on at his usual stone-breaking trot, and my offspring, in strenuous and entangled duet, declaimed to me the events of the afternoon.

It was without voice or warning that a row of men was materialised out of the darkness, under the Quaker's nose; they fell away to right and left, but one, as if stupefied, held on his way in the middle of the road. It is not easy to divert the Quaker from his course; we swung to the right, but the wing of the car, on my side, struck the man full in the chest. He fell as instantly and solidly as if he were a stone pillar, and, like a stone, he lay in the mud. Loud and inebriate howls rose from the others, and, as if in answer, came a long and distant shriek from an incoming train. Upon this, without bestowing an instant's further heed to their fallen comrade, the party took to their heels and ran to the station. It was all done in a dozen seconds; by the time the Quaker was pulled up we were alone with our victim, and Denis was hoarsely suggesting to me that it would be better to drive away at once. I have often since then regretted that I did not take his advice.

The victim was a very small man; Denis and I dragged him to the side of the road, and propped him up against the wall. He was of an alarming limpness, but there was a something reassuring in the reek of whisky that arose as I leaned over him, trying to diagnose his injuries by the aid of a succession of lighted matches. His head lay crookedly on his chest; he breathed heavily, but peacefully, and his limbs seemed un-injured. Denis, at my elbow, did not cease to assure me., tremulously, that there was nothing ailed the man, that he was a stranger, and that it would be as good for us to go home. Philippa, on the car strove as best she might with the unappeasable curiosity of her sons and with the pig-headed anxiety of the Quaker to get home to his dinner. At this juncture a voice, fifty yards away in the darkness, uplifted itself in song:

'Heaven's refle-hex! Killa-ar-ney!' it bawled hideously.

It fell as balm upon my ear, in its assurance of the proximity of Slipper.

'Sure I know the man well,' he said, shielding the flame of a match in his hand with practised skill. 'Wake up, me *bouchaleen*!' He shook him unmercifully. 'Open your eyes, darlin'!'

The invalid here showed signs of animation by uttering an incoherent but, as it seemed, a threatening roar. It lifted Denis as a feather is lifted by a wind, and wafted him to the Quaker's head, where he remained in strict attention to his duties. It also lifted Philippa.

'Is he very bad, do you think?' she murmured at my elbow. 'Shall I drive for the doctor?'

'Arrah, what docthor?' said Slipper magnificently. 'Give me a half a crown, Major, and I'll get him what meddyceen will answer him as good as any docthor! Lave him to me!' He shook him again. 'I'll regulate him!'

The victim here sat up, and shouted something about going home. He was undoubtedly very drunk. It seemed to me that Slipper's ministrations would be more suitable to the situation than mine, certainly than Philippa's. I administered the solatium; then I placed Denis on the box of the car with the bicycle lamp in his hand, and drove my family home.

After church next day we met Flurry Knox. He approached us with the green glint in his eye that told that game was on foot, whatever that game might be.

'Who bailed you out, Mrs Yeates?' he said solicitously. 'I heard you and the Major and Denis Leary were all in the lockup for furious driving and killing a man! I'm told he was anointed last night.'

Philippa directed what she believed to be a searching glance at Flurry's face of friendly concern.

'I don't believe a word of it!' she said dauntlessly, while a very becoming warmth in her complexion betrayed an inward qualm. 'Who told you?'

'The servants heard it at first Mass this morning; and Slipper had me late for church telling me about it. The fellow says if he lives he's going to take an action against the Major.'

I listened with, I hope, outward serenity. In dealings with Flurry Knox the possibility that he might be speaking the truth could never safely be lost sight of. It was also well to remember that he generally knew what the truth was.

I said loftily that there had been nothing the matter with the man but Christmas Eve, and inquired if Flurry knew his name and address.

'Of course I do,' said Flurry, 'he's one of those mountainy men that live up in the hill behind Aussolas. Oweneen the Sprat is the name he goes by, and he's the crossest little thief in the Barony. Never mind, Mrs Yeates, I'll see you get fair play in the dock!'

'How silly you are!' said Philippa; but I could see that she was shaken.

Whatever Flurry's servants may have heard at first Mass, was apparently equalled, if not excelled, by what Denis heard at second. He asked me next morning, with a gallant attempt at indifference, if I had had any word of 'the man-een.'

"Twas what the people were saying on the roads last night that he could have the law of us, and there was more was saying that he'd never do a day's good. Sure they say the backbone is cracked where the wheel of the car went over him! But didn't yourself and the misthress swear black and blue that the wheel never went next or nigh him? And didn't Michael say that there wasn't a Christmas this ten years that that one hadn't a head on him the size of a bullawawn with the len'th o' dhrink?'

In spite of the contributory negligence that might be assumed in the case of any one with this singular infirmity, I was not without a secret uneasiness. Two days afterwards I received a letter, written on copybook paper in a clerkly hand. It had the Aussolas post-mark, in addition to the imprint of various thumbs, and set forth the injuries inflicted by me and my driver on Owen Twohig on Christmas Eve, and finally, it demanded a compensation of twenty pounds for the same. Failing this satisfaction the law was threatened, but a hope was finally expressed that the honourable gentleman would not see a poor man wronged; it was, in fact, the familiar mixture of bluff and whine, and, as I said to Philippa, the Man-een (under which title he had passed into the domestic vocabulary) had of course got hold of a letter-writer to do the trick for him.

In the next day or so I met Flurry twice, and found him so rationally interested, and even concerned, about fresh versions of the accident that had cropped up, that I was moved to tell him of the incident of the letter. He looked serious, and said he would go up himself to see what was wrong with Oweneen.

117

He advised me to keep out of it for the present, as they might open their mouths too big.

The moon was high as I returned from this interview; when I wheeled my bicycle into the yard I found that the coach-house in which I was wont to stable it was locked; so also was the harness-room. Attempting to enter the house by the kitchen door I found it also was locked; a gabble of conversation prevailed within, and with the mounting indignation of one who hears but cannot make himself heard. I banged ferociously on the door. Silence fell, and Mrs Cadogan's voice implored Heaven's protection.

'Open the door!' I roared.

A windlike rush of petticoats followed, through which came sibilantly the words: 'Glory be to goodness! 'Tis the masther!'

The door opened, I found myself facing the entire strength of my establishment, including Denis, and augmented by Slipper.

'They told me you were asking after me, Major,' began Slipper descending respectfully from the kitchen table, on which he had been seated.

I noticed that Mrs Cadogan was ostentatiously holding her heart, and that Denis was shaking like the conventional aspen.

'What's all this about?' said I, looking round upon them. 'Why is the whole place locked up?'

'It was a little uneasy they were,' said Slipper, snatching the explanation from Mrs Cadogan with the determination of the skilled leader of conversation; 'I was telling them I seen two men below in the plantation, like they'd be watching out for someone, and poor Mr Leary here got a reeling in his head after I telling it – '

'Indeed the crayture was as white, now, as white as a masheroon!' broke in Mrs Cadogan, 'and we dhrew him in here to the fire till your honour came home.'

'Nonsense!' I said angrily; 'a couple of boys poaching rabbits! Upon my word, Slipper, you have very little to do coming here and frightening people for nothing.'

'What did I say?' demanded Slipper, dramatically facing his audience; 'only that I seen two men in the plantation. How would I know what business they had in it?'

'Ye said ye heard them whishling to each other like curlews through the wood,' faltered Denis, 'and sure that's the whishle them Twohigs has always – '

'Maybe it's whistling to the girls they were!' suggested Slipper, with an unabashed eye at Hannah.

I told him to come up with me to my office, and stalked from the kitchen, full of the comfortless wrath that has failed to find a suitable victim.

The interview in the office did not last long, nor was it in any way reassuring. Slipper, with the manner of the confederate who had waded shoulder to shoulder with me through gore, could only tell me that though he believed that there was nothing ailed the Man-een, he wouldn't say but what he might be severely hurted. That I wasn't gone five minutes before near a score of the Twohigs come leathering down out of the town in two ass-butts (this term indicates donkey-carts of the usual dimensions), and when Oweneen felt them coming, he let the most unmarciful screech, upon which Slipper, in just fear of the Twohigs, got over the wall, and executed a strategic retreat upon the railway station, leaving the Twohigs to carry away their wounded to the mountains. That for himself he had been going in dread of them ever since, and for no one else in the wide world would he have put a hand to one of them.

I preserved an unshaken front towards Slipper, and I was subsequently sarcastic and epigrammatic to Philippa on the subject of the curlews who were rabbiting in the plantation, but something that I justified to myself as a fear of Philippa's insatiable conscientiousness made me resolve that I would, without delay, go 'back in the mountain,' and interview Oweneen the Sprat.

New Year's Day favoured my purpose, bringing with it clear frost and iron roads, a day when even the misanthropic soul of a bicycle awakens into sympathy and geniality. I started in the sunny vigour of the early afternoon, I sailed up the hills with the effortless speed of a seagull, I free-wheeled down them with the dive of a swallow, and, as it seemed to me, with a good deal of its grace. Had Oweneen the Sprat had the luck to have met me, when, at the seventh milestone from Shreelane, I realised that I had beaten my own best time by seven minutes, he could practically have made his own terms. At that point, however, I had to leave the high road, and the mountain lane that ensued restored to me the judicial frame of mind. In the first twenty yards my bicycle was transformed from a swallow to an opinionated and semi-paralysed wheelbarrow; struggling in a species of dry watercourse I shoved it up the steep gradients of a large and brown country of heather and bog, silent save for contending voices of the streams. A family of goats, regarding me from a rocky mound, was the first hint of civilisation; a more reliable symptom presently advanced in the shape of a lean and hump-backed sow, who bestowed on me a side glance of tepid interest as she squeezed past.

The *bohireen* dropped, with a sudden twist to the right, and revealed a fold in the hillside, containing a half-dozen or so of little fields, crooked, and heavily walled, and nearly as many thatched cabins, flung about in the hollows as indiscriminately as the boulders upon the wastes outside. A group of children rose in front of me like a flight of starlings, and scudded with barefooted nimbleness to the shelter of the houses, in a pattering, fluttering stampede. I descended upon the nearest cabin of the colony. The door was shut; a heavy padlock linking two staples said Not at Home, and the nose of a dog showed in a hole above the sill, sniffing deeply and suspiciously. I remembered that the first of January was a holy-day, and that every man in the colony had doubtless betaken himself to the nearest village. The next cottage was some fifty yards away, and the faces of a couple of children peered at me round the corner of it. As I approached they vanished, but the door of the cabin was open, and the blue turf smoke breathed placidly outwards from it. The merciful frost had glazed the inevitable dirty pool in front of the door, and had made practicable the path beside it; I propped my bicycle against a rock, and projected into the dark interior an inquiry as to whether there was any one in.

I had to repeat it twice before a small old woman with white hair and a lemon-coloured face appeared; I asked her if she could tell me where Owen Twohig lived.

'Your honour's welcome,' she replied, tying the strings of her cap under her chin with wiry fingers, and eyeing me with concentrated shrewdness. I repeated the question.

She responded by begging me to come in and rest myself, for this was a cross place and a backwards place, and I should be famished with the cold – 'sure them little wheels dhraws the wind.'

I ignored this peculiarity of bicycles, and, not without exasperation, again asked for Owen Twohig.

'Are you Major Yeates, I beg your pardon?' I assented to what she knew as well as I did.

'Why then 'tis here he lives indeed, in this little house, and a poor place he have to live in. Sure he's my son, the crayture' – her voice at once ascended to the key of lamentation – 'faith, he didn't rise till to-day. Since Christmas Eve I didn't quinch light in the house with him stretched in the bed always, and not a bit passed his lips night or day, only one suppeen of whisky in its purity. Ye'd think the tongue would light out of his mouth with the heat, and ye'd see the blaze of darkness in his face! I hadn't as much life in me this morning as that I could wash my face!'

I replied that I wanted to speak to her son, and was in a hurry.

'He's not within, asthore, he's not within at all. He got the lend of a little donkey, and he went back the mountain to the bone-setter, to try could he straighten the leg with him.'

'Did Dr Hickey see him?' I demanded.

'Sure a wise woman came in from Finnaun, a' Stephen's Day,' pursued Mrs Twohig swiftly, 'and she bet three spits down on him, and she said it's what ailed him he had the Fallen Palate, with the dint o' the blow the car bet him in the poll, and that any one that have the Fallen Palate might be speechless for three months with it. She took three ribs of his hair then, and she was pulling them till she was in a passpiration, and in the latther end she pulled up the palate.' She paused and wiped her eyes with her apron. 'But the leg is what has him destroyed altogether; she told us we should keep sheep's butter rubbed to it in the place where the thrack o' the wheel is down in it.'

The blush of a frosty sunset was already in the sky, and the children who had fled before me had returned, reinforced by many others, to cluster in a whispering swarm round my bicycle, and to group themselves attentively in the rear of the conversation.

'Look here, Mrs Twohig,' I said, not as yet angry, but in useful proximity to it, 'I've had a letter from your son, and he and his friends have been trying to frighten my man, Denis Leary; he can come down and see me if he has anything to say, but you can tell him from me that I'm not going to stand this sort of thing!'

If the Widow Twohig had been voluble before, this pronouncement had the effect of bringing her down in spate. She instantly and at the top of her voice called heaven to witness her innocence, and the innocence of her 'little boy'; still at full cry, she sketched her blameless career, and the unmerited suffering that had ever pursued her and hers; how, during the past thirty years, she had been drooping over her little orphans, and how Oweneen, that was the only one she had left to do a hand's turn for her, would be 'under clutches' the longest day that he'd live. It was at about this point that I gave her five shillings. It was a thoroughly illogical act, but at the moment it seemed inevitable, and Mrs Twohig was good enough to accept it in the same spirit. I told her that I would send Dr Hickey to see her son (which had, it struck me, a somewhat stemming effect upon her eloquence), and I withdrew, still in magisterial displeasure. I must have been half-way down the lane before it was revealed to me that a future on crutches was what Mrs Twohig anticipated for her son.

By that night's post I wrote to Hickey, a strictly impartial letter, stating the position, and asking him to see Owen Twohig, and to let me have his professional opinion upon him. Philippa added a postcript, asking for a nerve tonic for the parlour-maid, a Dublin girl, who, since the affair of the curlews in the plantation, had lost all colour and appetite, and persisted in locking the hall door day and night, to the infinite annoyance of the dogs.

Next morning, while hurrying through an early breakfast, preparatory to starting for a distant Petty Sessions, I was told that Denis wished to speak to me at the hall door. This, as I before have had occasion to point out, boded affairs of the first importance. I proceeded to the hall door, and there found Denis, pale as the Lily Maid of Astolat, with three small fishes in his hand.

'There was one of thim before me in my bed lasht night!' he said in a hoarse and shaken whisper, 'and there was one in the windy in the harness-room, down on top o' me razor, and there was another nelt to the stable door with the nail of a horse's shoe.'

I made the natural suggestion that someone had done it for a joke.

'Thim's no joke, sir,' replied Denis, portentously, 'thim's Sprats!'

'Well, I'm quite aware of that,' I said, unmoved by what appeared to be the crushing significance of the statement.

'Oweneen the *Sprat!*' murmured Philippa, illuminatingly, emerging from the dining-room door with her cup of tea in her hand; 'it's Hannah, trying to frighten him!'

Hannah, the housemaid, was known to be the humorist of the household.

'He have a brother a smith, back in the mountain,' continued Denis, wrapping up the sprats and the nail in his handkerchief; ''twas for a token he put the nail in it. If he dhraws thim mountainy men down on me, I may as well go under the sod. It isn't yourself or the misthress they'll folly; it's meself' – he crept down the steps as deplorably as the Jackdaw of Rheims – 'and it's what Michael's after telling me, they have it all through the country that I said you should throw Twohig in the ditch, and it was good enough for the likes of him, and I said to Michael 'twas a lie for them, and that we cared him as tender as if he was our mother itself, and we'd have given the night to him only for the misthress that was roaring on the car, and no blame to her; sure the world knows the mother o' children has no courage!'

This drastic generality was unfortunately lost to my wife, as she had retired to hold a court of inquiry in the kitchen.

The inquiry elicited nothing beyond the fact that since Christmas Day Denis was 'using no food,' and that the kitchen, so far from indulging in practical jokes at his expense, had been instant throughout in sympathy, and in cups of strong tea, administered for the fortification of the nerves. All were obviously deeply moved by the incident of the sprats, the parlour-maid, indeed, having already locked herself into the pantry, through the door of which, on Philippa's approach, she gave warning hysterically.

The matter remained unexplained, and was not altogether to my liking. As I drove down the avenue, and saw Denis carefully close the yard gates after me, I determined that I would give Murray, the District Inspector of Police, a brief sketch of the state of affairs. I did not meet Murray, but, as it happened, this made no difference. Things were already advancing smoothly and inexorably towards their preordained conclusion.

I have since heard that none of the servants went to bed that night. They, including Denis, sat in the kitchen, with locked doors, drinking tea and reciting religious exercises; Maria, as a further precaution, being chained to the leg of the table. Their fears were in no degree allayed by the fact that nothing whatever occurred, and the most immediate result of the vigil was that my bath next morning boiled as it stood in the can, and dimmed the room with clouds of steam – a circumstance sufficiently rare in itself, and absolutely without precedent on Sunday morning. The next feature of the case was a letter at breakfast time from a gentleman signing himself 'Jas. Fitzmaurice.' He said that Dr Hickey having gone away for a fortnight's holiday, he (Fitzmaurice) was acting as his locum tenens. In that capacity he had opened my letter, and would go and see Twohig as soon as possible. He enclosed prescription for tonic as requested.

It was a threatening morning, and we did not go to church. I noticed that my wife's housekeeping *séance* was unusually prolonged, and even while I smoked and read the papers, I was travelling in my meditations to the point of determining that I would have a talk with the priest about all this infernal nonsense. When Philippa at length rejoined me, I found that she also had arrived at a conclusion, impelled thereto by the counsels of Mrs Cadogan, abetted by her own conscience.

Its result was that immediately after lunch, long before the Sunday roast beef had been slept off, I found myself carting precarious parcels – a jug, a bottle, a pudding-dish – to the inside car, in which Philippa had already placed herself, with a pair of blankets and various articles culled from my wardrobe (including a pair of boots to which I was sincerely attached). Denis, pale yellow in complexion and shrouded in gloom, was on the box, the Quaker was in the shafts. There was no rain, but the clouds hung black and low.

It was an expedition of purest charity; so Philippa explained to me over again as we drove away. She said nothing of propitiation or diplomacy. For my part I said nothing at all, but I reflected on the peculiar gifts of the Dublin parlour-maid in valeting me, and decided that it might be better to allow Philippa to run the show on her own lines, while I maintained an attitude of large-minded disapproval.

The blankets took up as much room in the car as a man; I had to hold in my hand a jug of partly jellified beef-tea. A sourer Lady Bountiful never set forth upon an errand of mercy.

To complete establishment – in the words of the *Gazette* – Maria and Minx, on the floor of the car, wrought and strove in ceaseless and objectless agitation, an infliction due to the ferocity of a female rival, who terrorised the high road within hail of my gates. I thanked Heaven that I had at least been firm about not taking the children; for the dogs, at all events, the moment of summary ejectment would arrive sooner or later.

Seven miles in an inside car are seven miles indeed. The hills that had run to meet my bicycle and glided away behind it now sat in their places to be crawled up and lumbered down, at such a pace as seemed good to the Quaker, whose appetite for the expedition was, if possible, less than that of his driver. Appetite was, indeed, the last thing suggested by the aspect of Denis. His drooping shoulders and deplorable countenance proclaimed apology and deprecation to the mountain-tops, and more especially the mountainy men. Looking back on it now, I recognise the greatness of the tribute to my valour and omnipotence that he should have consented thus to drive us into the heart of the enemy's country.

A steep slope, ending with a sharp turn through a cutting, reminded me that we were near the mountain *bohireen* that was our goal. I got out and walked up the hill, stiffly, because the cramp of the covered car was in my legs. Stiff though I was, I had outpaced the Quaker, and was near the top of the hill, when something that was apparently a brown croquet-ball rolled swiftly round the bend above me, charged into the rock wall of the cutting with a clang, and came on down the hill with a weight and venom unknown to croquet-balls. It sped past me, missed the Quaker by an uncommonly near shave, and went on its way, hotly pursued by two dogs, who, in the next twenty yards, discovered with horror that it was made of iron, a fact of which I was already aware.

I have always been as lenient as the law, and other circumstances, would allow towards the illegal game of 'bowling.' It consists in bowling an iron ball along a road, the object being to cover the greatest possible distance in a given number of bowls. It demands considerable strength and skill, and it is played with a zest much enhanced by its illegality and by its facilities as a medium for betting. The law forbids it, on account of its danger to the unsuspecting wayfarer, in consideration of which a scout is usually posted ahead to signal the approach of the police, and to give warning to passers-by. The mountainy men, trusting to their isolation, had neglected this precaution, with results that came near being serious to the Quaker, and filled with wrath, both personal and official, I took the hill at a vengeful run, so as to catch the bowler red-handed. At the turn in the cutting I met him face to face. As a matter of fact he nearly ran into my arms, and the yelp of agony with which he dodged my impending embrace is a lifelong possession. He was a very small man; he doubled like a rabbit, and bolted back towards a swarm of men who were following the fortunes of the game. He flitted over the wall by the roadside, and was away over the rocky hillside at a speed that even in my best days would have left me nowhere.

The swarm on the road melted; a good part of it was quietly absorbed by the lane up which I had dragged my bicycle two days before, the remainder, elaborately uninterested and respectable, in their dark blue Sunday clothes, strolled gravely in the opposite direction. A man on a bicycle met them, and dismounted to speak to the leaders. I wondered if he were a policeman in plain clothes on the prowl. He came on to meet me, leading his bicycle, and I perceived that a small black leather bag was strapped to the carrier. He was young, and apparently very hot.

'I beg your pardon,' he said in the accents of Dublin. 'I understand you're Major Yeates. I'm Dr Hickey's "Locum," and I've come out to see the man you wrote to me about. From what you said I thought it better to lose no time.' I was rather out of breath, but I expressed my sense of indebtedness.

'I think there must be some mistake,' went on the 'Locum.' 'I've just asked these men on the road where Owen Twohig lives, and one of them – the fellow they call Skipper, or some such name – said Owen Twohig was the little chap that's just after sprinting up the mountain. He seemed to think it was a great joke. I suppose you're sure Owen was the name?'

'Perfectly sure,' I said heavily.

The eyes of Dr Fitzmaurice had travelled past me, and were regarding with professional alertness something farther down the road. I followed their direction, dreamily, because in spirit I was far away, tracking Flurry Knox through deep places.

On the hither side of the rock cutting the covered car had come to a standstill. The reins had fallen from Denis's hands; he was obviously having the 'wakeness' appropriate to the crisis. Philippa, on the step below him, was proffering to him the jug of beef-tea and the bottle of port. He accepted the latter.

'He knows what's what!' said the 'Locum.'

From *Further Adventures of an Irish RM*

ANTI-SANTY

MARY BECKETT

Santa Claus wasn't around much in Belfast in the 1930s, but Father Christmas was, or Daddy Christmas for the little ones. And I believed in Father Christmas. I believed in God. I believed in my guardian angel. I was aware that, coming up to Christmas, my mother did not bring in her shopping to the kitchen table, but smuggled it upstairs. My two brothers, one a little older, one a little younger, were able to point out to me parcels appearing above the bookcase in the sitting room and on top of my parents' wardrobe. Parcels in those days were always wrapped in stout brown paper. They jeered at my gullibility. But I could not deny my faith – it's a very serious business in Belfast to deny one's faith. So I persevered in pretence.

The Christmas tree was dressed on Christmas Eve after we went to bed and the presents were laid out on our separate chairs in the sitting room. That door was shut until after we'd been to early Mass. There was no Midnight Mass in Belfast then. We walked home in the dark to a warm gaslit room and opened our presents. My parents were exceedingly generous.

It was well I had sorted out the whole business before I went to school at the age of six. For how could I have understood that while Father Christmas had brought me beautiful dolls, teasets, books and sweets, he brought the girls in my class a flat red stocking covered in white net holding 'novelties' to the value of a few pence. I who had plenty got more, while they who had little got nothing much. Why should Santa Claus behave in that way? How could that be explained to a child? By this time I understood quite clearly that there was no fairness of any kind in Belfast in the 1930s.

There is not a lot of fairness in Dublin either so my children were never to regard Santa Claus as anything but a joke. They knew we bought the presents and hid them until after Mass on Christmas morning when they followed, in their grandparents' house, the routine of my childhood. There is virtue in stability. Since we were responsible for the giving I was able to say 'No you can't have Scalectrix. There isn't room in the house to have it all laid out' or 'No you can't have a Sindy doll, because she is an abomination.' 'Wasn't she a horrible mother!' I hear you say. But I was the only mother they had. They were used to me. I always loved Christmas, loved buying presents, loved the sound of gold, frankincense and myrrh.

Babies are not found under cabbages any more. The days are gone when the stork brought them. Santa Claus belongs to that time. He is, the dictionary says, 'a fat white-bearded old man dressed in a red robe; an improbable source of improbable benefits.'

ELECTRICITY

VICTORIA WHITE

Four days before Christmas and the café was hung with paper
chains. Aisling was having her weekly treat, a cup of coffee
and a sandwich on her own in town. She was enjoying herself
very much. Every now and then she felt for her bag, where
her dole and her Christmas bonus lay hidden.

She saw him. He was coming towards her. How long was
it. Four years? Eamonn had the darkest hair and the bluest
eyes. For four years he had lived in her mythic past, when she
was sixteen and everything was new.

He saw her. 'Aisling?' He was smiling. She couldn't help
smiling back. He really seemed pleased to see her. 'You're
looking well.'

It wasn't true. She looked down.

'What are you doing with yourself these days?'

'Not much.'

He smiled. 'I don't believe that.'

Well, now she'd have to come out with everything. It was
always like this. She took a breath and said, 'I'm unemployed.
It's hard for me to get work. I had a baby a year after...I knew
you. I haven't got a chance to go back and do my Leaving
since. I can't afford to pay anyone to look after Julie. My
mother keeps her one day a week – dole day. I can't ask her
to do any more. She's getting on.'

She looked up and said strongly, 'Julie's lovely. I wouldn't have missed it for the world. I loved the father at the time, but he reacted really badly over me getting pregnant and I soon lost interest in him. I threw him out.'

She noticed he was still smiling at her and became embarrassed at the strength of her tone. He didn't need the lecture. He wasn't drawing back. 'So what about yourself?' she said, to break the silence.

Eamonn smiled. 'Oh, you know yourself. I'm between jobs.'

They both laughed, and he went on, 'I qualified as a teacher . . . Irish and music. I've never had a full-time job, just the odd few weeks filling in for teachers having babies and broadening their horizons. I love the job, but I suppose I'm going to have to think of something else. I'm still in debt from college.'

'You could go to England; they're crying out for teachers there.'

'But I don't want to go. I get the impression once I go there it's all over. I'll have to stay, I'll have responsibilities there. Anyway, I don't know why I should.' He smiled. 'Maybe I'm just too scared.'

He seemed different, softer, easier to talk to. Then he'd been a college student, full of himself and what he was going to do. There hadn't been any place for her in it all. It was just a few weeks one summer. But Aisling had always remembered it carefully as her one real experience of love.

'Will you have another coffee?' he said, and she said yes, and reached for her bag.

'Let me. I got my Christmas bonus today, it's my chance to treat a lady.'

Outside, the lunchtime shoppers dashed up and down the

street, battalions of women in high heels, men with their ties askew and newspapers in their hands. It was four days till Christmas and there was so much to be bought. Aisling and Eamonn were swept along the street by the tides of people and the electricity in the air. They were talking so much they hardly knew where they were. It had been so long since Aisling had talked to another adult, she kept marvelling – he understands! He understood everything, he knew what it was like. They could not keep walking along the street forever, and so they went into a pub and squeezed onto the red velvet seats, ordered hot whiskeys, then more hot whiskeys. Aisling's head was spinning, it could have been the whiskey and it could have been Eamonn.

'It's just the little things,' she was explaining. 'The sole on a shoe or Julie wanting to go to the pantomime . . .'

'I know,' he said. 'You could cope with it for a week, or maybe a fortnight . . . but then you just say to yourself, I need money, there are all these things just beyond my reach. Just a little money and they'd all be mine.'

'Everybody else having a decent Christmas, and you stuck in in your tatty old clothes. Who'd look at you anyway?' Aisling was getting tearful and angry. She was on her third whiskey.

Eamonn looked at her hard. He took her hand and said, 'I haven't been with anyone in so long.'

Aisling met his look and smiled. 'Neither have I.'

He leant over and kissed her and her body shuddered like an old car. 'You know what I'd like to do?' she said, after a moment. 'I'd like to have dinner in a restaurant. I've been dreaming of going to a restaurant. As my Christmas treat. To celebrate meeting up with you again.'

Because things would be different now. Maybe they could help each other find a job. Give each other strength and confidence. They walked out into the night among the fairy-lights and the shop windows. They had their arms round each other, and every now and then they kissed, and it was warm and soft. They crossed the Liffey and saw a restaurant with candles flickering at the tables and they went in. Eamonn was good at French and he ordered everything that took his fancy, making her laugh with his silly accent.

Aisling stretched back on the chair and gave herself to it. The food and the wine. Eamonn's eyes shining in the candle-light. She could feel her poor old body thawing and opening out again like a flower in water. And she knew her eyes were shining too, she could read it in Eamonn's. They ate as much as they could, until the waiter was laughing with them, and then they had liqueurs and coffee. Aisling touched Eamonn's knee then and said, 'Stay with me tonight.'

He said yes and she handed him her purse and told him to pay half of it, whatever it was, and not to let her know. And then they walked out into the frosty night and up Dame Street towards the house.

It was past midnight when they got back and Julie had been asleep a long time. Aisling touched her cheek and Eamonn smiled at her. Aisling's mother's snores filtered through from the other room and Aisling felt guilty for leaving her with the child for so long. But it was worth it. She would be better for Julie now, she was happier, not so resentful. They went downstairs and made up a bed on the sitting-room floor and sat a while by the electric fire warming their hands. They began to kiss and they realised how desperately they had needed the comfort of another body. The electric fire lit their smooth young bodies with orange warmth. They made love for a long time, until they were laughing at themselves and the battle between love and exhaustion. Aisling fell asleep with her head somewhere between Eamonn's chin and stomach, and Eamonn fell asleep with his arm around her.

The night hours were still. Stray dogs padded up and down the street sniffing for food. A joyrider tore up the street doing ninety. The night hours were cold. But the electric fire burned on and Aisling and Eamonn slept uncovered. The orange light contended with the dawn for a bit, but presently clean, blue light poured into the room.

Eamonn was dreaming about Aisling, living it through again. He slept deeply and when he woke eventually, shivering with cold, the clock on the mantelpiece said eight o'clock. He had to get out before Aisling's mother came down. He sat up quickly. Aisling wasn't there. He threw on his clothes and went into the kitchen. 'Aisling!'

She was sitting with her back to him. She did not turn.

'Aisling, love.'

He bent down to kiss her, but then he saw her shoulders were shaking. There was money spread out on the table, neat rows and piles of pounds and pence. She said, very quiet and even, 'You didn't tell me how much we spent.'

'You asked me not to.'

She turned then, furious, 'I had no idea. What am I going to do? I have to buy presents, food, shoes, clothes. I have a child to support.'

'I'll help you.'

'You've got nothing yourself.'

Eamonn was silent.

'It was the end of my Christmas, not the beginning.'

'We have each other.'

'What good is that. We can't bring Julie to bed with us. Jesus. Jesus.'

Then she clenched her fists and roared, 'We left the electric fire on all night.'

That was the last thing she ever said to him. She put her face down on the table and cried. She lashed out at him if he touched her, and it got late, so in the end he put on his coat and made to leave. He threw a fiver on to the kitchen table,

'For the electricity.'

But she turned round and stuffed it in his pocket, shivering with rage. He heard Julie call her mother then, and her quick, bright, hungry step on the stairs. And as there was nothing he could say, he let himself out into the bustling city.

YOUR MOTHER OWNED CHRISTMAS

GERALDINE DESMOND

The signs would be there for a while. Cellophane packages of raisins and sultanas and almonds piling up side by side. One weekend, we would find the kitchen table taken over by the big butter-coloured thick delft bowl, and by neat squares of waxed paper, onto which we grated steepled piles of suet or of breadcrumb, as we were ordered. We always skinned bits off our knuckles as we grated, and we always asked why the puddings and cakes had to be done so far in advance.

'They have to mature,' our mother would say, her hair wrapped in a scarf, to help her perm withstand the steam the boiling of the puddings would generate. 'The flavours have to meld into each other.'

Meld, we would murmur to ourselves. Meld. If it was a word, it was a pre-Christmas word, never used at any other time of the year. As we murmured the word we had been waiting for her to use, she would tell us again about the time that Nana, our great-grandmother, had mislaid a pudding after its first boiling and not found it until the following year.

'She gave it its second boiling then, and everybody agreed it was simply the best pudding any of us ever tasted,' she would say, turning over and over the ingredients in the big bowl with slow, sure, unhurried movements.

We never asked why, given that precedent, everybody didn't make their puddings a year in advance. We knew they would never survive the year if they hadn't been mislaid. We liked Christmas pud too much.

At that time, names and property might be inherited from a father, but Christmas was passed down the female line. Your mother owned Christmas. There was never a doubt about it.

It was your mother who, one day in early winter, would ask: 'What are you giving up for Advent?', the question carrying the assumption that you were giving up something, and it had better be a serious self-deprivation. Long before the psychologists talked about 'postponement of gratification', our mothers knew that the flavours of Christmas burst with particular vividness on taste-buds that had been having a thin time.

It was the same in the church, where, a few weeks before Christmas, one porch area would be curtained off with black sugar-paper which would be pulled aside on Christmas Eve to reveal the Holy Family and some shepherds all positioned around an empty centre area, looking (I used to think) in a manner inappropriately awed and affectionate towards a blank space where, on Christmas morning, the baby Jesus would be placed on a little straw crib, his hands raised to shoulder level as if acknowledging applause.

I always thought it was kind of tough on Our Lady to be left kneeling for days before she had a baby, but then the baby, when it made its appearance, wasn't like any baby I knew. It was always thin, the baby Jesus, with long slender six-month old limbs and a fine-boned knowing face. You never saw a baby Jesus that was crying, although sometimes you saw swaddled babies, tied up in white with criss-cross ribbons holding the cloth tight and the baby's arms and legs with it.

You'd find yourself surreptitiously stretching out your own arms and legs in sympathy with the cramped infant.

The three kings arrived a few days after Christmas and were ritually moved a bit closer each day thereafter. I insisted that the king carrying the gold (he happened to be black, in our house, and have a jewelled turban, rather than a crown) would be in first position, because I believed that he had his wits about him, whereas the other two were just wasting Our Lady's time. She's there in a stable trying to cope with a new baby, an old husband (Joseph, in almost all cribs, was white-haired and sort of hanging by one arm from a tall crozier thing as if he had no energy) a whole load of sheep and shepherds and a bright star that would let her get no sleep, and these three kings arrive with gifts. Gold she could certainly use, but *frankincense* and *myrrh?*

But there was a lesson in there, too. Our mother knew the lesson. The lesson was that you were grateful for any gift at Christmas, no matter how inappropriate. If your aunt gave you half a dozen wool vests, you behaved as if she had given you three puppies and a bike, throwing your arms around her and telling her how beautiful they were. I thought this was a cod, and I was sure that the slightly vague expression Our Lady had in every crib meant she was giving serious consideration, this Christmas, to pelting the two more dopey kings with their pressies.

In the last couple of days before Christmas, the house was filled with an excitement that was like bubbles in newly applied wallpaper. Our mother would pat down the excitement and it would just surface somewhere else, irritating our father, who was going through the Christmas lights one by one to find the one that was on strike and had brought out all its brothers.

The lights had to go on first, so while he did his diagnosis and rescue, we lifted the lids off the big flat cardboard boxes that had come down out of the attic, each filled with smaller boxes, each sub-divided like a noughts-and-crosses game with light card to keep the baubles separated and safe from each other.

The ornaments I liked best had been hand-made by my mother years before. A relative of ours in America had taken out a subscription for our mother to an American magazine called *Good Housekeeping*, which did lavish Christmas spreads, and one year they printed colour shapes which you were supposed to cut out and paste, one on either side of a piece of cardboard similarly shaped. Some were round, some oblong, some lantern-shaped. Our mother had neatly done this, threading strong silvered thread through the top of each. Out they came every year, with their round-mouthed carol singers and bell-wielding town criers of Pickwickian *embonpoint*, standing in snow, or skating on smooth ponds, hands tucked in muffs, scarves flying out behind them. One skater was downed – a child young enough to be portrayed with feet splayed, straight-legged in the air like a figure Y.

While we lined up the ornaments and put strings on the ones that had shed their loops, our mother sat at the kitchen table, gently pulling the long thin explosive bit out of the Christmas crackers. She did it as if she was de-stinging a bee, in deference to my terror of the things, which had resulted, one year, in a crying jag that had infected half the neighbourhood.

Ever since that, our Christmas crackers tore apart without a bang.

It was as if our mother had done a course in Christmas, and that only she knew the secret rules. In other houses, they didn't know the rules, and we allowed ourselves to feel quietly superior. Not knowing the rules meant putting your Christmas tree in the front window ('vulgar display'). Or putting balloons on the tree ('crude and out of proportion'). Or spraying the tree with glitter ('easier than proper decoration, but not as effective'). Our mother knew that a tree should have millions of little decorations, each in its pre-ordained place, lots of lametta, painstakingly hung, string by string, never thrown on in bundles, and a star at the top that looked into the room and didn't tilt to one side.

Our father was mostly a bit player during the holiday season. His moment of glory came when we had all written our letters to Santa, and he would tell us to throw them in the fire. Each Christmas, we did, expecting to see them destroyed by the flames, and each Christmas, with some trick of draught-management by quickly opening or closing a door, he ensured that they flew, unburned, straight up the chimney on their way to the North Pole.

But, it was our mother who defined, on Christmas morning, what was an 'absolutely ridiculous' but acceptably early time to get out of bed and start unwrapping, as opposed to what was actually still the middle of the night. Because the stockings were hung up downstairs, we had no way of knowing when Santa had arrived. The stockings were special, too. Our mother figured that ordinary stockings were no damn good for Santa purposes, so she knitted up a few, using a great deal of ribbing in the leg bit, and making each stocking fit to contain the leg of a small giant.

The ribbing meant that the stocking could expand at points to accept an oddly shaped item, and the end result was that on Christmas morning there was a deliberate 'postponement of gratification' as each of us turned our stocking around and around, noting the long shape that went from one side to another, as if a snake had swallowed a ruler sideways on, rather than longways, poking the softish box which seemed to have something round inside it, and – carefully – jolting the whole stocking up and down to hear the rattles.

Our mother was like a theatre director, managing every phase of the day. Although my father got to do the carving, it was like an audition, with my mother deciding whether he had done it well or badly. She decided all the moves. And the mood to go with them: the ticking off of a tantrum-thrower (always done in another room, so as not to taint the general atmosphere) or the cheering up of someone who had broken a vital part of a toy: all were her tasks.

She wore an apron most of the day. A special Christmas apron, white with broiderie anglaise around the rounded rim. Then, when evening came, the apron would be shed, and she would pick her way over and around the boxes and wrappings and the figure-of-eight railway tracks on the floor and sit on the piano stool. I would get to my place at one end of the piano and watch the big beautiful hands of her, spanning the octaves effortlessly, body bending to the music. Someone would turn out the room lights, so that at one end would be the crib with its star, at the other the sparky brightness of the Christmas tree and in the middle the glow of a dying fire. A touch of the keys and the voices knew which carol came next; the big men's voices asserting themselves for 'O Tannenbaum', the younger ones always singing 'Silent Night' in Irish, because we'd learned it at school, and my elder sister singing 'Scarlet Ribbons for Her Hair' as a solo.

It was our mother who permitted Christmas Day to start, and it was our mother who defined its end, allowing each of us to take with us one special toy, to sit on the floor beside the bed if it was awkwardly shaped or breakable, to be tucked in beside us if it was soft.

I HATE CHRISTMAS!

MARY ROSE CALLAGHAN

'I don't want a present this year,' my fifteen-year-old daughter announced, as I put the last touches to the tree.

'What?' I tripped over the fairy-light flex.

'I want money for Africa.'

Bronwyn's gear was total black – sloppy jeans and a man's jumper – emphasising her thinness. Both had been found in charity shops. Her skinny arms were now folded in scorn, as she glared at the winking tree.

'But it's Christmas,' I reasoned. 'Dad takes care of Africa.'

She tossed her long blonde hair. 'You mean he sends a measly cheque!'

'It may be measly but it's all we can afford.'

Her lip curled in scorn. 'Oh yeah?'

'Don't be rude.'

She laughed shortly, mimicking me. 'He's hardly *taking care of Africa.*'

I was struck dumb.

'Christmas is a waste!' my offspring pontificated. 'I hate it!'

'Never let me hear you say that.'

Suddenly my own mother was shaking her finger at me. Unlike Bronwyn I came from a big family. My parents were absolutely Dickensian about Christmas. In their palmy days they would start shopping in November, and every year about then a bulge would appear on top of the big wardrobe and every time the poor innocent adults went out, we devious children would play with the toys. The deception came to an end only when my brother pulled the wardrobe over, nearly smothering himself.

But my daughter had never known her grandmother, and couldn't see her now. She still pouted – the young are good at that. But, worried by her paleness, I coaxed, 'I'll get you something you really want.'

She wouldn't budge. 'I want the money.'

I lost patience. 'What about those hideous bovver boots?'

There, I had done it – put my foot in the boot. As well as ruining the surprise. Of course, our discussion flared into a row. Our discussions always did these days. According to Bron, I was a bitch. A fat one too. She promised to boycott the dinner. In fact she wouldn't eat *anything* on the day. We could stuff our faces. It was all we were good for. I said she could post her plate of turkey to Africa. She called me middle-aged and middle-class. We were both, her dad and I, overfed and over the hill. That was true. Two worn-out people – I ran a family as well as a drab job, while her father was an overworked accountant. Yes, it was the essence of blandness. But was I really a bitch?

Christmas is only a dinner and nothing but work, for mothers especially. This year, for once, I was ahead of the posse. I had the pudding and the brandy butter made. The turkey was ordered, the presents wrapped and ready for the tree. All I had needed were Bron's boots. I'd left her till last because, of my two, she's the more difficult to please.

And now she didn't want them.

I hated rows. But my daughter's idealism constantly provoked them. I didn't mind the Oxfam fasts or the sponsored walks for Romanian babies. But I had drawn the line at the parachute jump for paraplegics. It didn't make sense. What if she became one herself? That row had gone on for a week, but luckily she'd been disqualified on account of age.

On Christmas Eve I tried again. 'We'll go into town and you can pick out the boots.'

She tossed her head. 'No thanks, I'm busy.'

'You really don't want a present?'

'Please don't waste any more money, Mum.'

'Waste money? Since when have I wasted money?'

So I drove into town on my own.

'Oh, come all ye faithful . . . ' a group carolled in Rathmines.

But I didn't feel joyful or triumphant. Of course I cared about Africa. But Christmas was Christmas. Bron was getting boots whether she liked it or not. And she was eating turkey. I was worried about her thinness. She wouldn't touch red meat and brought an old Flora tub of brown rice or red beans to school. She was probably anaemic, as well as a budding anorexic. Many girls were. But were they all as rude to their mothers? It wasn't fair. How had I failed so miserably? Life was nothing but struggle. It was a conveyor belt that dumped you in middle age. You got there without knowing how.

I had meant to stop at the Swan Centre but found myself driving aimlessly down Harcourt Street. At the bottom, Bronwyn, wrapped in a red scarf, was carolling happily with a group of young people of all nationalities – Hispanics and blacks mingled with the pink Irish. Unlike our generation, they were so easy with one another. As the traffic slowed, I waved.

But seeing me, she looked away.

Oh, who would have children? At Bronwyn's age, I was stage-struck, while she was into groups with names like House of Pain.

I drove around the Green and parked in Harcourt Terrace in front of the recently renovated Palladian mansion in the middle of the street. The Christmas I was fifteen, my parents were renting its second-floor flat. I often made pilgrimages to the houses we lived in as children. It was a way of keeping in touch with my ghosts.

That was the year Benedict came for dinner. He was the only African I'd ever met. You hardly ever saw blacks in Dublin then. They seemed so exotic. The whole street was, and so far removed from the suburban estate I lived in now, where the Residents' Committee keeps pestering me about our hedges and the dogs. We hadn't a garden in Harcourt Terrace and nobody bothered about dogs. I stared up at the room where our spaniel had given birth to six pups. What had become of them? I didn't remember.

Just down the street lived Micheál Mac Liammóir. My mother had told me he had once played Heathcliff on the stage, and I had read *Wuthering Heights* four times and adored it. When I occasionally passed Micheál in the street, I stared in wonder, trying to look interesting. If only I could go on the stage. Once, appearing vaguely puzzled, he even tipped his trilby to me. Oh, glamour! And only a few doors away. But I was stuck in my own mundane existence, trying to cope with yet another Christmas.

Mostly past Christmases blur happily together. Books were

always under the tree, but I can't remember if the doll's pram was there when I was seven, or the nurse's uniform when I was six. Or vice versa.

If I remember a particular Christmas, it's because of some disaster. Like the time my brother got acute appendicitis in the middle of dinner. Or the time the turkey wouldn't cook. Or, of course, the time we had Benedict. That year, due to my father's illness, there wasn't much money, but this did not change my parents' basic philosophy.

In those days, the pillared house was still rather seedy. That year the six of us noisy children had piled home from boarding schools laughing and screaming at the top of our lungs and no doubt upsetting the other residents. Benedict, a Nigerian student I passed on the stairs with polite meaningless words, was one of them. Unlike today, people then didn't think of Africa being hungry. It was a place to convert. The home of missions and cuddly black babies. And Benedict.

He had coal-black skin and eyes that glittered in the dark and his greeting was ever the same – a formal 'How do you do?'

I always turned away shyly. What was he staring at?

So he concentrated on my young brother, once grabbing his trouser seat as he disappeared over the bannisters.

As he was so far from home, my parents naturally invited him for Chirstmas Day. I didn't see why they couldn't have invited Micheál Mac Liammóir. He, at least, was glamorous. But no, we were having Benedict.

Christmas came but once a year. So my mother, a night nurse, had arranged to work through the holiday and by hook or by crook everyone got a present. That year there were clothes and books for us older ones and toys for the younger ones. 'Am I getting my train set?' I still hear my small brother nag. My mother would only hum tantalisingly.

I'd nod, and, with a finger to my lips, point under the bed. With my mother, hope always triumphed over experience.

That year, an American aunt had sent me a cheque to buy a trenchcoat, the same as Audrey Hepburn wore. Unlike Bron, there was no question of my sending the money to famine relief. Like a sensible agnostic, I was wating for the sales. There was now only the dinner to buy. For which my mother could use her salary cheque. But on Christmas Eve morning she came home looking tireder than usual. 'I'm afraid they didn't pay me.'

'But didn't you ask them?' I quizzed.

My mother took off her coat and scarf. 'It horrifies me that a child of mine would expect me to dun people for money.'

'Asking them isn't dunning them.'

'It's hardly the spirit of Christmas. I'm afraid we'll have to use your money.'

I groaned. 'I hate Christmas. And what about my raincoat?'

She poked me in the ribs. 'Never say you hate Christmas! I'll find the money for your raincoat.'

I was fed up. 'You'll have to borrow it, I suppose.'

'Well, sharper than a serpent's tooth.'

I was not sharp at all. If today I'm out-generalled by my daughter, in those days it was my mother. It was no use. After all, we still had to have a turkey, and there was the matter of Benedict coming.

In those days, Findlater's of O'Connell Street still delivered.

They had all the necessities: a turkey, smoked ham, a Thompson's pudding, Club Orange and Jacob's Afternoon Tea. I watched resignedly as the blue-coated asssistant wrapped my money into a little casket which was carried by a wire to a cash desk on high. Goodbye, dear money. And later the change disappeared down a chute in Clery's, where we stopped for last-minute tree decorations. My mother thought having money on hand was uneconomical.

My older brother and I cooked the dinner and by mid-morning we had everything started. The ham was boiling away, the turkey stuffed and sizzling, the potatoes peeled, the sprouts ready and the tinned asparagus opened. There was now only the pudding to be heated and the brandy butter to be whipped.

At last Benedict knocked on the door.

My brother and I went to open it.

He was small and black, with a head appearing turtle-like out of a long drab overcoat. A bunch of flowers almost dwarfed him. He was probably quite young, but to me anyone at the university was ancient. Smiling, he gave the flowers to me.

I reddened in delight.

My brother drew him manfully in. 'Ah, you needn't bother with her.'

No one had ever given me flowers before. I put them in water in the kitchen. Then I spent the time till dinner cooking.

When everything was ready, we called my mother, who was getting some rest. Then we all sat ceremoniously at the carefully laid table under the gaudy paper decorations which trailed from each corner of the ceiling. My father said grace and carved the turkey. Then I served the vegetables while my brother poured the drinks. There was to be Club Orange for us children and wine for Benedict and my parents.

I was next to Benedict. And as soon as I sat down, a hand clutched my knee. I pushed it away, glaring. He just smiled dazzlingly, with his hundreds of brilliant teeth.

When we started eating a conversation got going, distracting him. He talked about Africa. Yes, he had been educated by the Holy Ghost Fathers. Yes, he found Ireland very lonely. And cold. Although the Irish people were very friendly. Hadn't he made new friends today?

And he smiled and pinched my knee again.

As my father served the pudding, he kept it up. This time I beat him off.

'What are you doing?' my father asked suspiciously.

Nonchalantly I waved my napkin. 'Eh, I just dropped this.'

'Hmm . . .' He gave me a curious look.

After dinner my father smoked his cigar. The smell still wafted over the years. Then he sang 'The snowy Breasted Pearl'. Then Benedict sang 'Oh, Come All Ye Faithful'. Then I recited Yeats's 'The Lake Isle of Innisfree'.

After that my brothers as usual wanted to play Monopoly but my mother favoured Elizabeth Taylor in *National Velvet* on the snowy TV. In our family the battle-lines were all strictly by gender. If the men wanted one thing, the women always wanted another. So I would usually side with my mother.

'I vote for Monopoly,' insisted my elder brother. 'Elizabeth Taylor's immoral.'

My mother reddened angrily. 'Why immoral?'

'Because she married about six times,' my brother said, with the pimply righteousness of seventeen.

'At least she married,' my mother snapped.

All this time Benedict was groping again.

'What do you think?' my mother said to me.

While I didn't admire Elizabeth Taylor's dexterity as much as my mother did, I quite liked the horse. Still, giving Benedict another kick, I said firmly, 'It's immoral to seduce people.'

My mother looked betrayed. 'Well, who would have children?'

'I know,' my father said placatingly. 'Benedict will have the casting vote.'

Benedict stood up, taking the napkin out of the V-neck of his jumper. 'I wish to thank you all very deeply. Also . . . I wish to explain . . . eh, in my country the customs are different.'

I wondered if they raped the hostesses there.

'It is the custom to have many wives. I am honoured to be giving the casting vote for Miss Taylor. I do not understand Monopoly.'

My brother groaned and my mother smiled triumphantly.

Imagination is memory, someone has written. Is the past really so happy or do we fool ourselves? Whatever the answer, memory sustains us. More than anything I wanted my children to have happy memories. Where was Benedict now? As far as I could remember he had been studying engineering all those years ago. Had he suffered the ravages of war and famine in Biafra? There had been so many disasters since – Somalia, the Sudan, Ethiopia, and this year, Rwanda. Catastrophies which we could barely imagine.

But you lived only one life and could only cope on a personal basis. My mother had understood that. Her love was always one-to-one.

The Legion of Mary moved into the house after us. And then the battered wives. Then it was a ruin for years. The windows were bricked up. Mottled patches of damp covered the pillars. Weeds choked the gravel. But somehow it was saved for today's plush and airy offices. Now all is changed utterly. A couple of houses down, Micheál Mac Liammóir is gone. But that day I didn't see well-dressed office workers. An aged actor sauntered towards me in a swinging camel coat, tipping his hat and smiling as he passed. In a chilly top room, a young African, huddled in a greatcoat, studied by a bar heater. My small brother's face pressed excitedly against the window. And I felt a ghostly poke: 'Never let me hear you say you hate Christmas.'

Christmas is for ghosts.

And Africa.

You have to make room for all. Of course, Bron was entitled to donate her present. I was lucky to have a child who cared. She was far less selfish that I was at her age. Maybe that's why we clashed so much. On Christmas morning she got her African cheque. She capitulated and ate her turkey – two helpings. And I found her some bovver boots in the sales.

CHRISTMAS IN OLD DUBLIN

ANNIE M. P. SMITHSON

Nowadays, when we think of Christmas, we associate the festival with turkeys, plum pudding, mince pies and so on. This kind of festival was practically unknown to our ancestors, and we undoubtedly got these notions from England.

The English fashion of keeping Christmas has changed through the centuries. We know that in the Middle Ages it was kept with great pomp and pageantry; in Puritan times it was forbidden to keep the festival at all, for it was regarded as a 'popish' feast. After the Restoration we may suppose that Christmas was again popular, but later on it must have fallen upon evil days, for one of the titles bestowed upon Charles Dickens by his countrymen was 'the man who discovered Christmas'. And most certainly his books, especially his famous *Christmas Carol* and *Christmas Stories*, did an immense amount to revive the keeping of the festival of Christmas in England.

We got the idea of the plum pudding and mince pies from England; from that country also – by the way of Germany, in the person of the Prince Consort – came the idea of the Christmas tree. I once spent a Christmas in the County of Donegal and found that plum pudding and mince pies were unknown amongst the people, and the children had never seen a Christmas tree.

One would like to visualise the first Christmas in Dublin after the introduction of Christianity. Was St Patrick there?

We know that he visited Dublin in the year 448, but we have no records that I know of relating to the keeping of Christmas in that year. But there is one thing certain, and that is, that the Feast would not have been so material a thing as it often is in these modern days. It would have been a great religious festival above all else; feasting and drinking would have taken a secondary place. Indeed, so far as we can gather from our history and records, at no time were the Gaelic people great eaters, not did they ever care for the pleasures of the table to the same extent as did the English.

We have proof of this fact when we come to the next Christmas I will mention. It is in the year of Our Lord 1171; Henry II has been excommunicated for his complicity in the murder of St Thomas à Becket, and has crossed to Ireland to spend his Christmas here. We are told that the Irish chieftains who were present at the royal feast were disgusted at the amount and quality of the food on the tables. They were particularly surprised to see the English eating the flesh of cranes, swans, and peacocks; they considered that such food as crane's flesh was not fit to eat. Henry caused to be built a great palace of wattlework, erected in the Irish fashion, and it stood where College Green is now. How strange to look backward and to try to imagine what Dublin looked like on that Christmas night of 1171.

Readers of *Sketches of Old Dublin*, by A. Peter, will remember the account of Christmas in Dublin in the year 1458. The big event in those days seems to have been the performance of the religious dramas called Miracle Plays. The Lord Deputy at that time was the Earl of Ossory, and he received an invitation from the citizens of Dublin to be present at a new play on every day of that week. Those were the days of the powerful City Guilds and these plays were all enacted by members of those Guilds. The performance took place in Hoggen Green – College Green as we now call it.

It should not be hard to draw a picture in our minds of Hoggen Green as it was in that Christmas of 1458. A large stage was erected and the open space before it was filled with spectators. Of course there was lots of room – the neighbourhood being almost open county then. For the Deputy and his friends, no doubt, special seats were reserved, but we can see the citizens, rich and poor, all striving to get a good view of the actors. What was the weather like? And which of us today would stand for hours – the plays were very long – in the open air in December to witness a play? And yet I suppose it might really be much healthier for us than sitting in the vitiated atmosphere of our theatres and picture-houses. Anyway, these ancestors of ours were hardy folk, and probably never bothered about weather conditions unless they were extreme altogether. Let us hope for their sakes that it was dry and frosty by day, with stars overhead at night, when they crowded to Hoggen Green to stare open-eyed at the players.

The Shoemakers acted the story of their patron, St Crispin; the Bakers gave a comedy in which the goddess of Corn appeared; the Smiths represented Vulcan in all his power; to the Carpenters fell the honour of portraying the story of the Nativity. One cannot but be struck with the extraordinary manner in which heathen mythology and the truths of Christianity were mixed together in those old plays. The queerest play of all, to my mind, was that of Adam and Eve, which was enacted by – of all people, the Guild of Tailors! After these plays were finished, others, dealing with incidents in the life of Our Lord and His Apostles, were ordered to be staged, by command of the Prior of All Hallows. Surely the citizens of Dublin had their full of theatrical displays in that Christmas week of 1458.

A PROPOSAL

JENNIFER JOHNSTON

Snow drifted slowly down through the bare branches of the trees. It floated into the light from the street lamps and landed and lay thinly on the statues, the few parked cars and filled the resting tramlines. The wide street was empty and very quiet. For once there were no drunks, tramps, tinkers or cabbies hunched about their half-starved horses to be seen. They had sensibly moved to whatever form of shelter was available to them, homes or doss-houses or holes in a wall somewhere. On the bridge, a tall cowboy in a ten-gallon hat and a small red Indian woman, boot-polish brown and feathers in her hair, were wrapped together in a large plaid rug. They leant on the balustrade of the bridge and stared sleepily down into the water. Flakes of snow hovered and then landed on the river's brown surface and then disappeared, absorbed, moved slowly towards the sea. The great clouds above were stained with the reflected light of the sleeping city.

'It's never proper snow,' complained the woman. 'Hardly ever. Thick crunchy snow like the icing sugar on a Christmas cake. It's hardly ever like that. We are deprived. It's most unfair.'

'I say, thank God.'

'We just get 'flu and chilblains and horrid east winds and red noses and filthy brown slush.'

The cowboy dropped a cigarette butt into the river. It

flashed for a moment as it fell, and then like the snowdrops disappeared.

'Me like heap snow. Me like heap big sleighs pulled by horses with jingling bells.'

'Christmas card stuff. Bumble, bumble.'

'How unromantic you are. Heap lot unromantic.'

There was a long silence. Up the river a bell rang half past something.

'The damp is starting to creep through the rug. My shoulders are getting damp. Heap damp.'

'Constance.'

There was an even longer silence. She moved uneasily under the rug, disengaging herself from contact with his warm body.

'What?'

'Would you marry me? I mean . . . would you . . . Well . . .?'

'No.'

'No?' His voice was slightly surprised. 'Just like that?'

'There's not much one can say . . . I mean . . . it's either yes or no, isn't it?'

'You haven't even thought about it. Think about it. Say that you'll think about it, please.'

'I don't have to think abut it. No.'

Another pause.

'But thank you just the same. Thank you, Bill.'

'What does thank you mean?'

'Oh hell, Bill, it means I can't think of anything else to say. It means thank you anyway for . . .'

'It . . . we could . . . Constance . . . why not?'

'Lots of reasons. I don't want to marry anyone. Anyone. It's not just you. I don't love you. No. Truly.'

'I though you loved me. I thought . . . we . . . you've . . . I love you very much.'

'I love you. I like you. But not the sort of love you mean. I'm sorry.'

She took his hand and squeezed it under the rug.

'Oh God,' she said, 'I hate this.'

She laughed abruptly.

'What a horrible thing to say. It just slipped out. Being a cause of misery doesn't appeal to me at all. I feel sick. Believe me Bill, dear Bill. I'd cause you real misery if I said yes. This at least will only be temporary.'

'Temporary.' He spoke the word with contempt.

'Me heap big trouble.'

The snow was transforming itself into needles of sleet. Not romantic in any way.

'Why do you say things like that about yourself? I know you. I know we could be happy.'

'Nobody knows that. Nobody knows anything . . . until perhaps it's too late. Me heap cold. Please take me home. Take heap big trouble home.'

He seemed hypnotised by the flowing water. For a moment the crazy thought entered her head that he might be contemplating suicide. She nudged him with her elbow.

'Bill.'

'I don't think you take me seriously,' he said gloomily.

'I do. I promise I do. And me, I take me seriously. You're behaving a bit badly. Why don't you take me seriously and believe me when I say no?'

'Because I don't think you know your own mind.'

'I'm learning about it. Feeling my way. The answer is no.' She pulled the rug from his shoulders and wrapped it round herself.

'No,' she said as she walked away across the bridge. 'No. No. No.' She didn't look back, because she knew that in his ten-gallon hat and his leather waistcoat, six-guns neatly balancing each other on his hips, he looked ludicrous, vulnerable and there was the terrible possibility that she might go back to him, through the brown slush and the sleet and put her arms around him and say, yes, safety, oh, yes. Yes.

From *The Christmas Tree*

THE DEAD MARKET

MAURA LAVERTY

The Dead Market was always held on the Monday of the week preceding Christmas Week. It was in full swing when I reached the town, and even before I came to the top of the bridge I could feel that unusual hum of activity. I could hardly wheel my bike through the higglers and women and creels of dead turkeys that crowded the market-place and overflowed onto the footpath at each side.

I was sorry to have missed the Live Market which had been held the previous Monday and at which Gran had sold her turkeys. I always found the Live Market an exhilarating affair because of the exciting high-pitched gobble kept up by the turkeys. Many of the women sold their birds at the Live Market, but more preferred to take a gamble on the price going up and they held on until the following week.

There was great good humour in the town.

The shopkeepers were pleased because the higglers' money would enable the women to settle their accounts. The women were happy because now at last they were to receive the reward of the exacting labours which turkey-raising entailed. For the birds were delicately-made creatures and difficult to rear. They had to be guarded more carefully than children against wettings and cold. Now at last they would get their money – twelve and fifteen and twenty pounds, some of them. They could pay their debts with their heads in the air and have enough left over for clothes and Christmas shopping. Their husbands, dressed in Sunday suits of shiny serge, had accompanied them into town just to make sure the money was not squandered. Most of the men had already had a pint or two and they wore a holiday look.

The children were highly delighted, too, for pennies flowed freely at the Dead Market. The stolid shy-eyed children from the far bog who, heavy-booted and trousered or frocked to below the calves, clung to their mothers' skirts, and the more daring town youngsters who dived in and out between the wheels of the creels – they would all come in for their share of the unaccustomed plenitude before the day was over.

I made slow progress for I knew everyone and kind enquiries for Gran and my mother and the rest of the family held me up at every step.

Anyway, it was difficult to detach oneself from the various entertainments that were part of the Market. The Fairy Broy was there with his bunch of song sheets. A grizzled little man as gnarled as one of the trees in the rath, the Fairy looked at least a hundred. But he had a voice that could lift the thatch off a house. He had his mouth open now and was letting his voice out in one of his ballads in a way that drowned every other noise. The Fairy was doing his best to entice an audience away from his rival, a fellow whom we had never seen before in Ballyderrig. The novelty of the stranger's act out-weighed the Fairy's best vocal efforts. Presently he realised that he was fighting a losing battle. He closed his toothless white-bearded mouth on an ear-splitting note and philosophically joined the crowd that had gathered around the newcomer.

The stranger was a Strong Man. A huge brawny fellow

with a big stomach and thighs like the trunk of a tree. He had a small bullet head that was as bald as a baby's, and when he took off his coat and handed it to his assistant, a tired-looking wisp of a woman in a black shawl, he rolled up his shirt sleeves and flexed his muscles in a way that made us all gasp.

Our eyes nearly popped out of our heads at the feats that followed. He lifted enormous weights as if they were sods of turf. He lay down and laid a slab of stone on his chest and let the men hammer it to smithereens on his bare flesh without turning a hair.

I had to clear off when the woman started coming around with the cap because I only had the ten-shilling note for the messages. I felt mean and dishonest about not paying for the entertainment I had enjoyed, and when I had bought my goods and had plenty of ready change I came out looking for her. I was just in time to see the two of them disappear into Johnny Dunne's bar. I could not very well follow them there, so I let it go at that.

The pig was killed by the time I got home. The carcass was lying on the floor of the washhouse which was streaming with the water that had been used for the scalding. The pig was covered with clean sacks to keep in the steam and make scraping easier.

Johnny Dooley, Britches and Mike Brophy were in the kitchen having a meal of tea, bread-and-butter and blue duck eggs. An unusually frugal meal for Derrymore House, but it was merely intended as a stop-gap until the evening when they would be given a supper worthy of their labours, for the hardest part of the work was yet to come. Mrs Noone stood at the far end of the table stirring salt in a basinful of the pig's blood for black pudding.

'How did the turkeys go?' Gran demanded when I came in.

'Ninepence ha'penny a pound, Gran. Mrs Joe Flynn got tenpence for hers.'

'Good,' Gran commented with satisfaction. 'They're down instead of up. I'm glad I got rid of mine last week.'

When this meal was finished, the men went back to the washhouse to scrape the pig. When all his bristles were scraped away and he was pale and smooth and naked-looking they would hang him up and disembowel him. The boning and curing would be done next day when he was cold and the lard was set.

In the meantime there were the heart and liver and stomach to be brought into Gran and the intestines to be washed and left soaking in cold salted water to make casings for the puddings.

Gran and Mrs Noone were in their element that evening. So were Judy and myself as we bustled around helping them. There were a hundred things to do. The heart to be cleaned and stuffed with potatoes and onions and sage and set to roast in the baker. The liver to be divided up, a portion for Mrs Noone, one for Granny Lynn, one for Britches. Our own share of the liver to be sliced, rolled in flour and fried with bacon in the big iron pan. Oatmeal to be toasted for the black and white puddings, and the stomach to be scrubbed for Mrs Noone to take home. She knew how to make a tasty dish of it by packing it with stuffing, stitching it up and roasting it.

Judy Ryan brought in an armful of early cabbage from the garden. Clusters of frost diamonds nestled in the wrinkles of its green leaves. And presently Mike Brophy came in with a bucket of potatoes which he had washed under the pump by churning them around in the icy water with a fork-handle.

When the potatoes and the cabbage were cooked, Mrs Noone made colcannon by mashing them together with plenty of butter, a naggin of milk and pepper and salt.

And at last they were ready.

There was a supper!

Pale green colcannon light and fluffy as bog-cotton and floating in good rich gravy. Slices of brown liver, crispy on the outside as new-baked crust, but inside all tender and blood-pitted and sweet. Juicy cuts of heart saturated with flavour from the savoury stuffing. And the stuffing itself! Soul of onion, breath of thyme and smoothness of potato. That stuffing caressed your palate and glided lovingly down your throat to find a resting place, not in your stomach but in your heart's core, warming its very cockles.

'Well, I'm glad to have that inside me shirt,' Britches said at last, pushing back his plate. 'An' now I'll be off for I'm goin' to ould Jimmy Doyle's wake.'

'And is he dead then?' asked Gran, whose face wore the proud contented expression of the artist who has laboured to produce a masterpiece, and who has seen the results of his skill and inspiration favourably received by the critics.

'Did you not hear, ma'am? He dropped dead half-an-hour after comin' out of second Mass yesterday mornin'!'

'The Lord have mercy on him,' said Gran, to which we all answered 'Amen.'

Sure enough when I was in the town that morning I had noticed the shutters on the shops. When anyone went from us in Ballyderrig, every shopkeeper put up one shutter as a mark of respect for the dead.

'It should be a powerful wake,' Britches said.

'Why? Did The Roach make a good collection?' asked Mrs Noone, referring to our custom of burying our poor by means of public subscription.

'He did that,' John Dooley said morosely, speaking for the first time that evening. 'He got a ten-shillin'-note out of me.'

'It should be a powerful wake entirely,' Britches persisted. 'I was talkin' to Dinny Mulpeter in the town this mornin' an' he told me The Roach spent most of the money on a half-barrel of porter. An' I believe he could well do this, for what he spent on the coffin was harmless. Like cardboard, Dinny, says it is. It'll be the mercy of God if poor ould Doyle doesn't fall through it on the way to the graveyard.'

'No fear of that, Britches,' Mike Brophy said. 'It won't take a very strong coffin to carry poor ould Jimmy. He was light enough, God knows. Sure he was no bigger than a dog's diddy – an' that's a small piece of mate.'

Next morning the men returned to cut down the pig and cure him. Mrs Noone came, too, for the main part of the cooking was still to be done – lard to be rendered, puddings to be made and the brawn to be prepared and cooked and moulded.

About twelve o'clock, Britches came into the kitchen with a basin heaped with the fillets and spare ribs and griskins - those juicy sweet little trimmings from the sides which it would have been a crime to salt. Before setting about making a griskin and rib stew for the dinner. Gran put a good share of both on one side for Mrs Noone.

Later the casings were brought in clean and wet and viscous from their bath in salt water. We hung them to dry over the back of a chair near the fire. Judy hung the big pot on the crane to boil while Gran and Mrs Noone and myself prepared the filling for the puddings. Toasted oatmeal, boiled chopped onions, chopped lard and plenty of pepper and salt, this was the filling for the white puddings. The same mixture with the addition of the pig's blood and a little milk was used for the black puddings.

When the intestines were dry the real work of the pudding-making commenced. We took the half-yard length of pig-gut and tied it at one end with string. Then we blew it open with our mouths so as to get in the filling. This was eased down to the end until the gut was filled to a length of nine inches, care being taken to pack the mixture loosely to allow it room to swell. The end of the pudding was then made secure with string. An inch or so further up the gut was tied again and a second pudding was made in the same way. A snip of the scissors between the two separated them. When all the filling was used up, Mrs Noone took one of Gran's sharp steel stocking needles and prodded the puddings here and there so that they would not burst in the boiling. Then into the pot with them to simmer and bubble for half-an-hour or so, after which they were lifted out and hung in the buttery to dry – fragrant promises of the treat that would accompany the breakfast rashers of ourselves and our neighbours for the next week.

When that was done we turned our attention to the brawn. Britches brought us in the feet and the head chopped in two.

'You scrub the feet, Delia,' Gran said to me. There was her kindness again. She allotted me that easy job to save me having any part in the unpleasant work of cleaning the head.

The brains were taken out to be flanked and put by for the following morning, when they would be parboiled, coated in batter and fried as an extra tid-bit with our rashers and puddings. The ears had to be cleaned and singed and the nostrils rendered immaculate with a sharp knife – cleaning out the snoggles, Mrs Noone called it. In our house we liked our brawn salty, so Judy got down the big pickling crock. She rubbed the head and feet with a mixture of salt and saltpetre and put it in the crock to pickle until the next day, when it would be boiled with pepper and onions and spices until it was almost jelly. After this the meat would be lifted from the bones, cut small and packed with a little of the liquor into bowls to set firm. A plate would be put over each bowlful with an iron standing on each plate. When set, it cut into delicious transparent pink slices, spicy and meaty.

We had the stew for dinner. For supper we had the fillets, sliced and pounded and fried and lardy cakes.

There was never anything in the world like Gran's lardy cakes. Golden-brown and pancake thin, you spread butter on them just as they came from the griddle. If you were toothless as the Fairy Broy you could enjoy those lardy cakes, for their mouth-watering flakes melted on your tongue.

'There are the easiest things in the world to bake,' Gran often said to those who praised her lardy cakes. 'Flour and sheet lard and a good pinch of salt. Roll them thin and bake them quick.'

It would be a mistake to let the apparent simplicity of this recipe fool you into trying to bake lardy cakes like hers. Many additional ingredients would be needed to make lardy cakes taste like those I devoured in Derrymore House that night. For they would need to be baked by the kindly old hands that had given you every happiness you had ever known. They would need to be eaten under the wise loving eyes of one for whom you felt the perfect and abiding love. And, as you ate them, your heart would have to be filled with the peace and wellbeing which attend a completely happy home-coming.

We had been so busy all day that we had completely forgotten the wake. Mike Brophy remembered it when John Dooley and Britches stood up to go home.

'How did the wake go, Britches?' he asked. 'For a man who's been up all night doin' away with a half-barrel of porther you're lookin' purty fair.'

Britches spat contemptuously into the fire.

He struggled for words - or to suppress words.

'The curse of hell on the drop of porther that ever passed me lips last night,' he said. 'It's the back of me hands to the Roach Doyle from now on. He's the lousiest, mangiest, stingiest ould get that ever came out of the Bawn.'

'Why? What happened?' asked Gran

'You'll hardly credit this, Mrs Lacy, but when meself an' Lar Casey an' Luke Heavey an' a few of the lads went to the wake, that ould bags – savin' your presence – had the door locked. Aye, an' wouldn't open it!'

'That was a queer way to hold a wake,' Mrs Noone said.

'But wait till you hear. We looked in through the window an' there was the Dummy Foy an' himself an' they guzzlin' porther for dear life. Barrin' the corpse, not one but themselves there.'

'Did you knock?'

'Did we knock, is it? Did we nearly kick the – ' Realising that his description of the door and of what they nearly did to it might offend Gran's ears, Britches checked his tongue with obvious difficulty. 'Yes, we knocked. But that ould feck-me-la didn't open the door and ask us in decent like any Christian. What does he do? He opens the window the dawshiest little bit an' says, 'Go home, lads. This is a private wake.' He shut it right in our faces an' back with himself an' the Dummy to the porther. An' the rest of us got sweet damall of it.'

The recollection of his deprivation brought such bitterness to his usually sunny heart that Britches took his cap abruptly from behind the door, and off with him into the town to seek company where a man might express his grievances freely and untrammelled. But the rest of us thought it a good joke, for that was the first time we had heard of a private wake.

The Roach Doyle – that wretch whom I hated on Annabel Gorry's account – had added to our vocabulary, for thereafter whenever any selfish inhospitable gathering took place, the people of Ballyderrig referred to it scathingly as 'a private wake.'

From *Never No More*

THE AUSTRALIAN WOMAN

KATE CRUISE O'BRIEN

On Christmas Eve the sky fell in. Mum was in the kitchen cooking. On Christmas Eve Mum boils the spiced beef. She rolls out the Jus-Rol puffed pasty and makes mince pies.

'Homemade, how are you,' she snarls. 'I make better pastry than his mother ever did because I use Jus-Rol. They could try that in an ad. They could also tell you that it's slavishness that counts as Christmas. It's not the pastry. It's the pain. I hate pastry and flour and rolling-pins but they haven't invented a mince pie that can be homemade without them. Yuch!' And Mum, being Mum, sprays flour all over the kitchen floor. On the other hand Mum tunes in to the Christmas carols on the radio. I've seen her cry into the flour when the solo boy soprano starts with 'Once in Royal David's City.' Mum sings along in her thready little voice, worn out with too much smoking.

Anyway this Christmas Eve, Mum was baking and boiling and crying and having, as far as I could tell, a perfectly splendid time, when the bell rang.

'Antonia!' roared Mum.

I was up watching television. There isn't room for anybody else in the kitchen when Mum starts on her Christmas Eve stint. And Mum won't have television in the kitchen. She says that the radio leaves her hands free but I think she wants would-be TV watchers out of her way. She does a lot of dreaming, does Mum with her radio. You can just see her making pictures in her head. But she doesn't like being interrupted so she's installed this ship's bell in the hall which she clangs if anyone has the nerve to ring the front doorbell. *I'm* supposed to answer the front door when I hear the ship's bell. It clanged. I opened the front door. There was this little blonde woman standing on the step. She was crying. She was thin, very thin and wearing a fur coat. A fur coat! Think of all the poor animals. Actually I rarely do. I mean I eat meat and walk on leather, for heaven's sake. But there was something terrible and pathetic about this little lady standing in our porch wearing fur when that's simply not done anymore and obviously she didn't know it. And her tears were making white tracks down her poor, thin, over-made up face.

'Come in,' I said.

'I don't want to bother you. It's a bad time to come, Christmas Eve. Is your Mum in?'

She wasn't Dad's Blonde. That was clear. She was blonde all right but her voice was Australian, and not confident Australian like you hear on *Neighbours*. It had a whining cringe to it. Dad likes women who stand up to him. Also he's a snob. He'd never go for an over-made-up peroxide blonde with the wrong sort of accent. This woman looked like someone Mum would like because obviously she had problems. Mum isn't ever snobbish about problems or about anything else.

'Mum's in,' I said. 'She's crying in the kitchen.' I dragged the woman in. 'Mum's crying because it's Christmas and she always gets het up about Mary and the manger.' I was gabbing and rushing because, suddenly, I knew who this woman must be. This was Brian's wife. As Mum would say, who else could it be?

'Mum,' I said as I opened the kitchen door, 'Mum, this is a woman who wants to see you.'

Mum was red-eyed and flour-spattered. 'Oh,' she said.

'I said to your daughter I didn't want to bother you,' said the woman in a quick, fussy voice. 'I know it's Christmas and I'm sorta desperate. I came to spend Christmas here with my husband and he isn't *here*!'

And then she sat down at the kitchen table and started sobbing as if her heart would break.

'Oh dear, oh dear,' said Mum rushing across and patting the woman's fur shoulders with her floury hands. 'Oh dear. Husbands rarely are where they're supposed to be, particularly on Christmas Eve,' she said with a baleful look at the clock. Dad had been working lunch at the hotel this Christmas Eve. He should have been back hours, well one hour, ago.

'Who is your husband?' asked Mum. 'And why should he be here?'

'Not here in this house,' said the woman, sounding irritated. 'Here in *Dublin*. I went to his hotel. He wasn't there. He said he would be there but he wasn't. He told me about your family in his letters. He said you'd been "A home from home".' He doesn't like home so I suppose there's a woman about. He thought the home business would make me feel better. It didn't, you know. The more lies he tells the more details he gives. The details are always OK. He has no imagination,' she said as if that made it worse. 'But the story is always wrong. The story is never true.'

'Did you come from Australia?' I asked. 'All that way?'

'No I did *not*! Did he tell you that? I did not. I'm a British citizen. I live in Birmingham. With him. Well I sometimes live with him. I did come from Australia. Brisbane as-a-matter-of-fact.' She said it all in one gulp. 'I wish I'd stayed there.'

'Well you can always go back if you want to,' said Mum calmly. I could see that she was thinking about kangaroos and flying doctors. She's always loved the thought of Australia. 'All that space,' she says dreamily as if she could see the tiny figures of Dad and me diminishing on a fading skyline.

'But you must tell me who you are?'

'You mean you don't know?' It seems snobbish to tell it the way she said it, 'You mean yu don't naow?'

'No,' said Mum. 'I don't.'

'You let a perfect stranger in out of the night to cry on your Christmas table and you don't know!' (I can't do the naow bit again.) 'You don't know! Your daughter knows. All that talk of Australia. *She* knows.'

'You're Brian's wife,' I said. I felt witch-like, like Mum in her black hat. Is magic hereditary? But of course, as Mum always says, it isn't magic. It's simply guess-work, based on fact. And I was fairly sure that Mum had known this was Brian's wife as soon as she came through the door. Mum, for some reason, was stalling.

'I'm Brian's wife,' said the woman, 'I'm Marie. How do you do?' And she held out her hand to Mum, who grasped it in her own floury paw.

'Pleased to meet you,' she said. Perhaps she did watch *Neighbours* in her spare moments.

'I'm Brian's wife,' said Marie. 'But what I want to know is where Brian is and what sort of story did he tell you?' At this point there was the sound of mighty rushing wind, which meant someone had opened the front door. There was a crash (door slamming) and a stumble.

'I'm drunk!' carolled Dad from the hall. 'I'm very very drunk. I've been drinking and drinking and drinking since lunchtime and now I'd like to pinch a fat lady's bottom. Where is my wife, my moderately fat wife. Not that her bottom is fat. It's just her middle.'

'Do you have to put up with that all the time?' said Marie, sounding awed.

'Not often,' said Mum who'd got the giggles. 'Not half often enough. I'm the one who drinks around here. He only gets festive once every decade. I think he must have taken to the Leeson Street strip and got involved with too many Tequila Sunrises. He's a very innocent drinker. He thinks sweet is safe. Don't mind him. He's quite harmless.'

'Oh-my-God!' said Marie.

. . .

It was six o'clock on Christmas morning. There was a truly horrid sound from upstairs. Dad was being sick. Mum had left him a bucket so it was none of my business anyway. I flipped up the blind and looked out. It was still and quiet and peaceful. Just a few lights on in the road. Perhaps there were children rustling around under Christmas trees. I felt suddenly homesick for the way it had been. Stockings and stars and excitement in the morning. Aunt Grace coming at eleven, with, always, the most magic present of all. I wandered into the dining-room to look at the tree. This was my time in the house. The time when I owned it. There, under the tree, was the most enormous big box, a big crude cardboard box covered with ivy, the blackened sort which grew on the wall outside the dining-room. The ivy had been sprayed silver over the black and there was this notice on the front: For Antonia From Santa. It's not when people are nasty to you that you want to cry. It's often when they're suddenly, unexpectedly, nice.

Santa had left a lot of presents for Antonia. Sweets and oranges, books, the best sort. Mum is very good at books. No scarves, which I hate, but two of those games which bubble and tumble in plastic before your eyes. From Dad, I guessed. And two tapes. Not Strauss waltzes or Beethoven, the only kind of classical music Mum can stand. Early Christmas music, breathing prayer, the kind that Dad likes and I like which is odd since we're both much less naturally religious than Mum is. I mean none of us believes in God but Mum still lights candles in darkened churches and thinks it will work. 'You weren't even reared a Catholic,' says Dad, who was. 'That's why,' says Mum. At the bottom of the box there was this other little box. A black, velvet, rectangular box. On the top of the box there was a kind of cat's cradle of sticky-tape, grimy tape, enclosing a white envelope. Fairly white. Mum never could manage parcels. Inside was a card:

> *Dear Antonia,*
> *When I was fifteen my godmother gave me these*
> *pearls. I'm handing them on to you because I love*
> *you. I know, I know you'd hate me to mention it but*

I do anyway.
Much love, Elizabeth. . .Your Mother.

I was kneeling, gloating over these treasures when Marie came in. She'd stayed the night.

'We can't send her away,' Mum had said. 'It would be far too much like no room at the inn.'

Actually I thought Marie would have stayed even if we'd tried to throw her out. Marie was the staying sort.

The dining-room was cold. We don't have central heating. We just turn on gas fires – there's one in almost every room – when we want to stay in a room. Most of the time we stay colder than other people. The hall is nearly always frigid.

The spare room is worse than frigid.

'Hey!' said Maria. 'Is this Santa's stocking? Look at the box with the silver ivy on it. That's beautiful. You *know*.'

I did know.

'It's funny,' said Marie. 'How you miss the things you never had. My Mum, Maw we called her, died when I was little. Dad was a good sort of bloke. There was always a present for every one of us at Christmas – but never anything like this. Maybe it's the climate,' she said, shivering in Mum's old summer dressing-gown. 'Christmas isn't the same at home. When it's that hot you don't really get to believe in Santa and sleigh-bells. Never missed it really until Birmingham. After I got married in Birmingham I got to understand about Santa. I couldn't wait to have a baby and a Christmas tree.' Marie had taken off the make-up and tied up her hair. She looked now like an elderly, tired child. 'We got the Christmas tree. It's green plastic and I take it out every year. The baby never came. Your Mum's lucky.'

'Yes,' I said. I could feel the pressure building in Marie's fiddling. She was tidying up wrappings, picking tinsel off the carpet . . . quick, nervous, waiting. She was going to ask a question and I was going to have to answer it.

'Who's Brian's woman, Antonia? Like I said to your Mum, he never did go in for family life. So if he's seeing your family there has to be a woman there, somewhere. It's not your Mum. I wouldn't ask if I thought that. Your Mum isn't that sort of lady.'

'What sort?' I asked, feeling vaguely insulted on Mum's behalf.

'Your Mum's straight,' said Marie. 'Brian likes something more complicated. If he'd wanted straight he would have stuck to me. Brian likes what he can't have. Not someone who would say that. But someone who wouldn't.'

'It sounds complicated,' I said.

'No it isn't,' insisted Marie. 'It's kind of obvious once you know how. He wants to make someone reject him and then he can blame his failure on them He's one of nature's willing victims.' And she grinned. 'So who's the lady in the case? It's not going to hurt *that much*. It's not the first time. But I need to know.'

The trouble was that I knew that it was going to hurt much more than *that much*. A lady, straight or complicated, is one thing. A baby is another.

But this was Christmas day and Grandma was going to be here, as sure as God made little apples (did he?) at four o'clock. Someone was going to have to answer Marie's question, sooner or later. It might as well be me.

'It's my Aunt Grace,' I said in a gabble. 'She's having a baby. We all think it's his baby. But she won't see him and she doesn't seem to want to marry him or anything like that. Mum would kill me if she knew I'd told you this, but someone had to, didn't they?'

'Someone did have to,' said Marie slowly.

Dad said it was all my fault. From the way he said it you'd think that Marie had slit her wrists open in the bath or gone down to the canal to drown like a dog. In fact Marie stayed pretty calm. She just kept saying 'I want that baby!' over and over again. Mum didn't say it was my fault. Mum is keener on small sins like not doing the washing up, than she is on big ones. She says she feels too guilty to contemplate any moral failure that isn't strictly measurable. 'In other people, that is,' she once said. 'I was born with the certain knowledge of my own sin so I find it difficult to think about other people's. I'm sure I'm much guiltier than anyone else can possibly be.' But Dad doesn't seem to suffer from guilt. Not that sort of guilt anyway. I think he thinks that life is pretty simple. That's the Catholic in him. Mum behaves as if there are very few sins – except her own – just constant muddle. But Dad has a tidy mind. He thinks he can track down a sinner – not that he'd call anyone that – and make sense of the muddle.

'Why did you tell Marie about Grace, Antonia?' Dad kept on saying. 'Did you have to do that? Did you want to hurt Grace? To pay her back. Did she hurt you that badly?'

'Oh for God's sake!' said Mum.

'I just told Marie the truth!' I roared. I hate Dad when he tries to get psychological. I don't like people trying to wander about in my mind. 'Did you want to have Christmas dinner with Grandma wondering who this was and Marie being humiliated when Grandma found out? 'Oh but Brian can't be married, dear, my daughter Grace is having his baby.' I can just hear her, can't you? You're a big ass! Marie was going to find out anyway. How long did you want her to wait? Until you could be polite about it? She asked me a direct question and I gave her a direct answer and I don't know why you have to make such a big deal about it. I can't understand why you want me to feel wrong about it. It was honourable to tell her. Perhaps you can't imagine that,' I said sarcastically. 'A sense of honour?' I was being a bit histrionic, I knew, but it felt good. 'You don't lie to guests in your house, I just told her the truth, that's all.'

'I have to think that this was manipulative,' said Dad, unmoved by my passion.

'Oh my God,' said Mum again.

If anyone was manipulative, Marie was. She'd declared herself, now she hung around. When I say that she was manipulative, I don't mean to say that I didn't like her. I did. But she had the sort of staying presence that weak people often have. She occupied our spare room, possibly the coldest room on earth. The spare room has no heater or gas fire and it has, as far as I can see, no ventilation either. When Mum sleeps in there the room reeks of cigarette smoke in the morning and she has to open the window wide to air the place. Mum explained all this to Marie. She could stay, but . . . but the room was cold and it wasn't ventilated so you should really, said Mum, sleep with the window open. No you couldn't use an electric fire because of our ancient wiring and the fact that the only socket in the room was a light socket.

'Not,' said Mum, 'a power-point.'

We have a big house. It should have four big bedrooms. But Mum turned one of them into a sitting-room and the other into her study. So there's only one cold, mouldy, smelly spare room.

'People can come to stay,' says Mum, 'but they don't stay long.' Marie showed every sign of being the exception to this rule.

On Christmas Day, after what Dad called my 'Unnecessary and Untimely Revelations,' Marie tactfully disappeared around one o'clock and avoided both Grandma and Christmas dinner. This turned out to be a smart move. Christmas dinner was pretty horrible. Mum was distracted, Grandma was angry in a suspicious sort of way and Dad, well Dad was plain sick. When he cut into the turkey he discovered that the inside was mostly raw because Mum had spent the morning dealing with my Unnecessary and Untimely etc. and listening to Marie wittering on about how she wanted this baby and trying not to answer her questions about Grace. What did Grace look like and where did she live were the main ones. Marie kept on asking if Grace had a better figure than she, Marie, did. I thought this was ridiculous because Marie didn't have what you could call a figure at all. She was just straight up and down and not very much of that, as Grandma would say. But Mum said vaguely that she'd never really thought about Grace having a figure because she was always so preoccupied with her own and now that she came to think of it, the last time she'd noticed that Grace had any shape at all was in 1976 when they both went swimming at Seapoint. 'It was quite sunny that day,' said Mum helpfully, 'and Grace was thinner than I was, taller too, of course, but then she always is. That was the day I realised that I'd have to give up wearing a bikini. It was just after Antonia, of course. I'd got a bit flabby, no stretch marks though,' said Mum with pride. 'Since then Grace took to the layered look. She's tall, I do know that. She's not fat, I think, but all those clothes make her look bulky.'

As for Grace's address, since Mum didn't know where Grace was definitely or for certain, she wasn't prepared to give Marie an address. 'It's difficult, you see,' said Mum looking earnest. 'She's an unmarried mother – well, will be – and a teacher. I can't have people making enquiries at her flat.'

All of this was complete gobbledegook but it was so mad and pseudo-logical and wrapped up in meaningless innuendo that Marie gave up and said that she'd go to the hotel and collect her luggage and see if Brian had turned up or left a message and please, could she stay another night with us if he hadn't done either of those things?

'I feel at home here,' she said pleadingly.

There is nothing stronger than people who can admit to being weak.

'You and Brian both,' said Mum a trifle bitterly, thinking, no doubt, of the beer. And then she went into this unwelcoming routine about the spare room, which didn't seem to deter Marie one bit.

So, after Marie had gone, Mum put the turkey in the oven

and forgot to turn on the gas, which meant, of course, that when Dad cut into the golden skin he found raw flesh underneath.

'Some of it must be cooked,' said Mum. 'I remembered I forgot at least two hours ago.'

'There *is* a layer of cooked flesh,' admitted Dad. 'But the rest . . .

'Well let's eat the cooked part and ignore the rest,' said Mum snappily. I could see she was getting angry. After all she'd had to deal with my Unnecessary etc., and Marie too, while Dad was still sleeping.

'Oh EEElizabeth,' said Grandma, 'forgive me. I can't eat raw flesh or even cooked meat that's been in contact with raw meat. I read something about it in *The Irish Times* the other day. Salmonella or some such thing. The fact is that raw and cooked don't mix.'

Grandma was wearing a pink paper hat. We'd had the crackers while Mum was crashing around the kitchen trying to convince herself that the turkey was cooked. The trimmings were wonderful. They usually are. Sprouts and chestnut stuffing and mushroom gravy. Mum is very good at trimmings. She's just not very good at meat.

'It's so boring,' she says. 'If you watch it it doesn't get cooked and if you don't watch it, it gets burnt.'

Maybe Mum hadn't been stonewalling with Marie. Maybe she is mad and illogical and full of meaningless innuendo.

'Anyway,' said Mum, 'It's mixing *cold* raw and cooked meats in supermarkets and delicatessens that's the problem. And they have to be different kinds of meats too. How could a turkey argue with itself?'

Dad put down the carving-knife.

'I'm very sorry, everyone, I don't feel well,' he said and charged out the door. Mum persuaded Grandma to have trimmings and Grandma volunteered to 'try a little skin, dear, just so as not to hurt your feelings.'

Grandma stirred the food around the plate with a fork. She didn't eat much but then she never does. The end of the meal was a relief.

'Well,' said Mum as I took away the plates, 'Let's get drunk. Have some port everyone?'

From *The Homesick Garden*

FROST FIGURES

HONOR DUFF

The weather that December morning was appropriate to Nora's mood as she walked in her cold silent garden which overnight had become petrified by hoar frost.

She tried to remind herself that frost was only frozen dew as her boots crunched on the rimed grass leading to a small promontory at the end of the garden. In clear weather it served as a viewing plarform, but today sea-fog had net-curtained all vision.

It was impossible to see the outline of Bray Head to the south where Cathy, her youngest daughter, lived by choice with a group of strangers. These people had convinced her errant child that parental love and family were of base coinage, to be rejected in favour of their own newly minted currency.

The once-fastidious Cathy now lived with people who didn't wash very much, ate food that looked like hens' droppings and mandrake roots, and whose mesmeric leader was an obese Eastern patriarch with knowing eyes and a white stretch limo.

Alan, Nora's husband, had advised against taking drastic action.

'She's over twenty-one. She'll hate us for forcing her to come back – which I doubt we can — and we might end up losing her altogether.'

'But if they brainwash her?' Nora said tearfully. 'And then all that free love must have them rotten with disease.'

'Cathy is basically a sensible girl. She'll see them for what they are – eventually,' Alan had reassured her

'If she was sensible she wouldn't have taken up with them in the first place,' Nora had observed.

'Look, love, it's like the early Christians,' Alan had argued. 'They were all for communal love, secret signs and symbols, and people used to say, "See how these Christians love one another!" But you've only to read St Paul to see that they were far from perfect – quarrelling among themselves, complaining, disobeying orders. In fact just like the rest of us clay-footed breed.'

The foghorn groaned like some Ice Age mammoth in travail as she turned next to gaze in the general direction of the city, in the inner depths of which Peter, her youngest son, and so recently a schoolboy, had been caught up by a German Valkyrie, ten years or so his senior, and carried off, if not to Valhalla, then to a flat in the aptly named Liberties. Peter had decided to skip that adolescent no-man's-land of angst, acne and giggly girls and instead had marched to the front line of passion and straightaway surrendered.

'You bloody pup, you're hardly out of short trousers and yet you think you can set up a love nest with a woman. What about your studies, what about your future, what about your mother?' Alan had raged at a white-faced but stubborn Peter who had come back to collect his things.

Nora shivered and drew her dressing-gown around her. Although held fast in its crystalline prison, the garden knew it would eventually be released. Nature was only playing dead, playing possum. In spring those blackened branches would sprout an amazing display of pretty pink flowers and green leaves like an ancient American matron candy-flossed in pastels.

She looked back at the house, solid and beautiful, open to all available light yet protected by sentinel trees. Too big now for just the two of them but they would not leave, not yet, maybe never. Her eldest daughter, Nuala, with her increasing brood, might want to live here one day, but David, her eldest son, and his wife, Carol, preferred to be closer to the city.

Walking back to the house she gathered some frosted pine cones and slipped them into her pockets. A watery sun trying to pierce the fog had made the iced twigs of a silver birch sparkle. She remembered she needed to buy some more Christmas decorations.

Alan was on his second cup of coffee, hunched over a book on the kitchen table. Since retiring, he had pledged to read all the books he had never had time for and was at present working his way through Thomas Hardy. He winced as she let cold air into the warm kitchen.

'You'll get your death going out in a dressing-gown,' he scolded.

She poured herself coffee and walked to the window. 'It's beautiful out, more mysterious than snow, somehow.'

'I'll take your word for it,' Alan smiled.

'Do you remember in the old days there used to be marvellous designs in ice on the glass, shapes like ferns if there was frost and patterns like flowers if it had been raining?'

'Nothing marvellous about scraping the ice from your window, chilblains on your feet and hands, frozen pipes, sheer misery. No, dear, I don't want the good old days without central heating,' Alan said, turning a page.

She ignored him and went on. 'Those shapes are called frost figures and are made from six-rayed star crystals. Each ray or arm is set at exactly sixty degrees of an angle to its neighbour.' He looked at her in surprise and she laughed. 'I read that once in a child's encyclopedia and never forgot it.'

'People forget the mathematical precision of nature,' Alan said. 'Everything mapped out, nothing left to chance.'

Nora sighed and rinsed out her cup. 'Listen, Alan, I've decided not to have them all here for Christmas Day dinner. I want a quiet meal with the two of us. They can come in the morning for the present-giving and drinks – that will be sufficient.' She sat down again and waited for his reaction.

'Are you not well, dear? he asked worriedly, and at the concern in his face, she smiled and said, 'No, I'm just tired and heartsick over those two defectors. I'm really not up to a big effort.'

'Would you like to go to a hotel?' he enquired.

'Absolutely not,' she said firmly.

'As long as you're not sick,' he said, still worried.

'I'm sick cooking gigantic turkeys every year. Last Christmas I felt like the witch in *Hansel and Gretel* trying to push it into the oven.'

'What about the pudding?' he asked anxiously.

Every Christmas she made a huge plum pudding to his mother's recipe. Tied into a larded calico cloth, it was cooked for endless hours in a black cauldron which wouldn't have looked out of place on the stage of the Abbey. The final product, pumpkin-shaped and decorated with a sprig of berried holly, was like a comic-book pudding, something to be tackled in one go by Desperate Dan.

'I'll do a smaller one in a bowl,' she promised.

'You're making changes,' he said sadly. 'I hate changes.'

She looked at his disappointed face and smiled. 'You looked like Peter just now,' she said. 'I'm going to ring Nuala and tell her the change of plans. You know, Nuala says that the two youngest were spoiled compared with herself and David. She says they got it too easy when life was more prosperous for us, particularly after your early retirement.'

'Nuala knows it all,' he grumbled. 'Wait till her lot grow up and give herself and Tony hell.'

'I know,' she answered. 'It's so safe and happy when they're all little, gathered around the table or blissfully asleep and you can look in on them on the night watch and know all is well.'

She began to cry softly and he went around the table and held her to him, stroking her hair and comforting her with low, murmuring words of reassurance.

Christmas Day was mild and unseasonably sunny. Nora suggested that she and Alan go for a walk before the one o'clock arrival of her children and grandchildren. Alan was stirring a container of mulled wine, tasting and adding to it. The kitchen was warm and aromatic with roast turkey and spicy odours.

'Have we time?' he asked reluctantly.

'Yes,' she said firmly, 'or you'll have that tasted away.'

They were putting on their coats in the hall when they heard someone fumbling with a key in the lock. They stared as Cathy came through the door. She was wearing a series of layered garments and her red hair was excaping from a knitted hat. Her face looked swollen and dirty and her hands were purple with the cold.

'My God, Cathy!' Alan rushed forward and folded her to him. Nora stood rigidly, holding herself back, feeling as she used to when any of them got lost in town, wanting to slap her and hug her at the same time.

'Are you just here for the day?' she managed to ask her now sobbing daughter.

'Oh no, I want to stay! I'm just exhausted. I've walked miles and hitched lifts. My feet are sore and I want to sit down.'

Alan supported her into the kitchen and she sat down gratefully before continuing. 'It was terrible there, you've no idea . . . '

'All right, love, just be quiet now, you're home and safe.' Alan took off her stained boots and thick socks and examined her blistered feet tenderly.

'I'll run you a bath,' Nora said. 'You look as if you need it.'

'Will she let me stay?' Cathy whispered to her father when Nora had left the room.

'Don't be silly, pet, of course she will. Your mother is just as delighted as I am to see you, even if she doesn't show it.'

'Well, I just want to have a wash and then sleep. Can we talk later?' she asked, yawning.

'As long as you don't wash and go, that's OK by me,' he said with a grin.

'Oh, Dad, I've missed you, and even your corny jokes,' Cathy said, just as Nora returned and asked her if she was hungry.

'I just want to sleep,' Cathy said nervously, looking at Nora, who, seeing that look, walked over and embraced her daughter.

'Welcome home, love,' Nora said. 'Now go and have your bath.'

Cathy smiled radiantly at both of them and went upstairs.

'What do you make of that?' Nora asked Alan.

'Let's not ask her any questions just yet. No recriminations either, or promises. She's worn out physically and emotionally.'

'But if she takes off again after Christmas, I won't be able to bear it,' Nora said.

'She's here, she's safe for today and we've the others to think of,' Alan said, going over to the container of mulled wine and pouring them each a glass. 'It's the best Christmas gift of all. Cheers!'

Cathy's voice interrupted them, calling down that there might be a group of people following her but she didn't want to see them or talk to them and could her father please handle it?

He shouted up reassurances as Nora protested. 'Now we have to suffer a raiding party surrounding our house on Christmas Day, after that rip putting us through all kinds of hell these last weeks. And she had the nerve to let herself in with a key!' she added as an afterthought.

'Why?' Alan smiled. 'Were you going to turn her away? You know you can't turn anyone away on Christmas Day. It's a universal rule, like your six-rayed frost figures.'

'I presume that doesn't apply to members of strange sects?' Nora asked sarcastically.

'It certainly does not,' Alan said grimly, going to the phone and asking his son-in-law Tony to bring his cricket bat when visiting.

Nora checked on the trays of glasses, dishes of crisps, nuts and savouries, and put another pine log on the fire. The room looked lovely with the firelight and pale winter sky reflecting on the blonde-gold wood inside. She had put bowls of Christmas Roses on high shelves out of reach of little hands. The tree was overdressed and gaudy, groaning with three sets of coloured lights and every decoration Henry Street could offer. Carol and David had a restrained two-colour tree with some hand-carved German ornaments, but the children loved her tinselly creation and so, to tell the truth, did she.

When the two cars arrived, disgorging shrieking children, adults and a barking dog, she forgot about the dreaded visitors, but Alan called Tony and David aside for a conference.

About an hour later the doorbell rang and Alan opened it to a young man and two girls. They asked politely for Cathy and, still politely, insisted on waiting for her. Alan told them to leave and when they refused, he called Tony and David.

Tony came out hefting a cricket bat, his six-foot-something frame filling the doorway. Behind came David with the metal rod from a vacuum cleaner.

'Physical violence on Christmas Day?' the man mocked. 'No peace and goodwill, then?'

Alan told him he was trespassing and the group finally walked slowly up the driveway, stopping every now and then to argue.

Inside, Nuala told Carol to keep the children in, took a curved ornamental dagger from the wall and released Brandy. He leaped barking at the intruders and Nuala ran up to the men, brandishing her weapon.

'She's my sister too,' she snapped at David when he told her to go back.

Nora peeped in at Cathy, who was still soundly asleep, and, seeing the commotion in the driveway, ran downstairs and took a large iron pan from the shelf. She ran to join the others, clanging it off the rocks for effect.

'You're all mad,' the spokesman said, shaking his head. He paused again outside the driveway and announced that since they were obliged to leave private property, the would sit here in their parked car on the public highway and wait for Cathy.

Tony walked around the car and kicked at the tyres. 'Your treads are in a pretty bad way and the guards around here are hot on that. And look to your rear light,' he said.

'What about it?' the man asked, walking to the back of the car.

'It's broken,' Tony said, tipping it with the cricket bat. 'And on these dark roads that's lethal. Better drive away now before it gets dark.'

The man looked at the little group. 'Some Christians, using violence to attain your ends.'

'I'll attain *your* ends if you don't get into this car immediately!' Nora said, raising the frying pan.

'She'll come back to us. We're her real family,' one of the girls said before getting into the car. They drove off to cheers from the group, who danced around the road in triumph.

"Twas a famous victory,' Alan said, 'even though I only used verbal weaponry. And Nuala, put that thing away before you damage someone with it.'

'It's not fair, Dad. She's only a girl and she got a dagger and I only got this,' David whined in a pretend little-boy voice, holding up the vacuum cleaner part. Nuala leaped at him, pretending to stab him, and he ran down the driveway to be met halfway by the excited children who had broken out from Carol's ineffectual custody.

'Oh God, Alan, Mrs Coughlan is looking out her window. Wave to her as if everything is normal,' said Nora, hiding the pan behind her back and waving with her free hand.

Alan put his arm around Tony and Nora. 'Let's go in and celebrate the rout of the barbarians,' he said, laughing.

Once back at the house, Nuala called her mother aside and told her that she and Tony had invited Peter and Helga to Christmas dinner in their house.

'Well, that's your own business,' her mother replied coldly.

'Actually, Mum, I asked them to call in here on the way to our place; it's Christmas Day and you should make it up with Peter.'

'You had no right, Nuala,' Nora said angrily. 'I'm not receiving that woman under my roof, Christmas Day or not, and by the way, I'm sick of people expecting me to put up with all sorts of awful people and things just because it's Christmas Day!' She cleared debris off some plates and slammed down the lid of the pedal bin.

'Will I get you a brandy?' Nuala asked. 'You're getting very upset.'

'No, I don't want a brandy. I'm going to turn off the oven and go to bed for the rest of the day or maybe I'll turn up the oven, take the turkey out and put my head in instead,' her mother snapped.

'Look, Mum, I know he's a young brat, but it's a passing phase; you mustn't break contact with him.'

'You sound like a TV counsellor,' Nora said angrily. 'As far as I'm concerned, that woman pounced on him like a . . . like a she-wolf and carried him off to her lair.'

'Peter and the She-Wolf,' Nuala giggled, then apologised when she saw Nora's face.

'I'm going for a walk in the garden and nobody is to follow me,' Nora ordered, putting on a jacket that was hanging behind the door.

'You're not going to jump off the cliff, I hope,' Nuala said in mock-panic, but Nora didn't answer and went into the garden where the light was fading and the house, brightly lit, stood like a beacon against the coming darkness.

Her children and Alan were standing at the window looking out, pointing at the lights across the bay, pretending they were not watching her.

One time, she thought, I was a young girl running to meet Alan on a winter's night, when the moon had silver-plated the earth and the frost reflected back its light so that I was bathed in white radiance. Alan had said their love would endure because it had been forged in hard winter conditions, no theatrical aids like summer sunshine, birdsong and flowers. It had been a long journey from that time to now, and still strange to realise she was responsible for the existence of so many of those loved figures behind the glass.

Peter found her under the trees but stopped a few feet away.

'Happy Christmas, Mum,' he said hesitantly. His face looked white and strained and she wanted to cry out to him 'Are you hurt my son, are you hurt at all?' like the mother in the fairy story whose son had cut out her heart for his girlfriend, then fallen while running with it.

Instead she took his face between her hands and said, 'Happy Christmas, Peter,' and kissed him. The figures at the window smiled and turned away.

Nora linked his arm and said, 'Come on, love, let's go back inside to the warmth.'

BIOGRAPHICAL NOTES

CECIL FRANCIS ALEXANDER
Born County Wicklow 1818 but spent most of her adult life in the north of Ireland. Her most famous hymns, including 'Once in Royal David's City' and 'All Things Bright and Beautiful' were written for her Sunday School in Strabane. She died in 1895 in Derry, where her husband was bishop.

MARY BECKETT
Born Belfast 1926. Author of a novel, *Give Them Stones* (1987), and two collections of short stories as well as children's books.

MAEVE BINCHY
Born Dalkey, County Dublin, 1940. Journalist and author, she has published five novels, several collections of short stories and television plays.

MARY ROSE CALLAGHAN
Born Dublin 1944. She has published three novels, a biography of Kitty O'Shea and a novel for teenagers.

ANNE DEVLIN
Born Belfast 1951. Short story writer and playwright. Won the Hennessy Award in 1982 and has won several awards for her plays. She has published one volume of plays and one collection of short stories, *The Way-Paver*.

HONOR DUFF
Born Dublin 1938. Her stories have been published in anthologies and periodicals and broadcast on radio. She has also written radio scripts.

JENNIFER JOHNSTON

Born Dublin 1930. Novelist and playwright. She has published seven novels, including *The Captains and the Kings*, and several plays.

MAURA LAVERTY

Born in County Kildare 1907. Novelist, journalist, broadcaster, she published several novels, cookery books and books for young people. She died in 1966.

PATRICIA LYNCH

Born Cork 1898. Suffragist, journalist and novelist, she published over fifty books, including many classic children's titles. She died in 1972.

MOY MCCRORY

Born Liverpool 1953 of Irish parents. She has published two collections of short stories.

VAL MULKERNS

Born Dublin 1925. She has published four novels and three collections of short stories.

KATE CRUISE O'BRIEN

Born Dublin 1948. She has published one novel and one collection of short stories, *A Gift Horse*, which won the Rooney Prize. She also won a Hennessy Literary Award.

TERRY PRONE

Born Dublin 1949, she is the author of several books on communications and personal management and one collection of short stories.

CELIA SALKELD

Born Dublin. She was an actress with the Abbey Theatre and RTE Repertory.

ANNIE M. P. SMITHSON

Born Dublin 1873. Published many successful romantic and

nationalistic novels, including *The Marriage of Nurse Harding*. Died in 1948.

PEIG SAYERS
Born 1873 in west Kerry. She published two autobiographical volumes in Irish. She died in 1958.

SOMERVILLE EDITH Œ
E Œ Somerville was born in Corfu in 1858. She lived in west Cork and collaborated with 'Martin Ross', her cousin Violet Martin (1861–1915) to produce several collections of short stories and novels.

VICTORIA WHITE
Born Dublin 1962. Journalist and critic. She has published one collection of short stories.

ACKNOWLEDGEMENTS

For permission to reprint the stories specified, we are indebted to:

Mary Beckett, 'Anti-Santy', © Mary Beckett 1994. By permission of the author.

Maeve Binchy, Exract from *Light a Penny Candle* (Century Publishing), © Maeve Binchy 1982. Reprinted by permission of Century Publishing Ltd.

Mary Rose Callaghan, 'I Hate Christmas!', © Mary Rose Callaghan 1994. By permission of the author.

Geraldine Desmond, 'Your Mother Made Christmas', © Geraldine Desmond 1994. By permission of the author.

Anne Devlin, 'The Journey to Somewhere Else' from *The Way-Paver* (Faber and Faber) © Anne Devlin 1986. Reprinted by permission of Shiel Land Associates Ltd.

Honor Duff, 'Frost Figures', © Honor Duff 1994. By permission of the author.

Jennifer Johnston, Extract from *The Christmas Tree* (Hamish Hamilton), © Jennifer Johnston, 1981. Reprinted by permission of the author.

Maura Laverty, Extract from *Never No More* (Longmans; reprinted Virago Press), © Maura Laverty 1942. Reprinted by permission of David Higham Associates Ltd.

Patricia Lynch, 'Last Bus for Christmas' from *The Genius*, © Patricia Lynch. Reprinted by permission of the estate of Patricia Lynch.